THE MIAMIS!

THE MIAMIS!

Nancy Niblack Baxter

Hoosier Heritage Series

1987
Guild Press of Indiana
6000 Sunset Lane, Indianapolis

ISBN: 0-9617367-3-9

TABLE OF CONTENTS

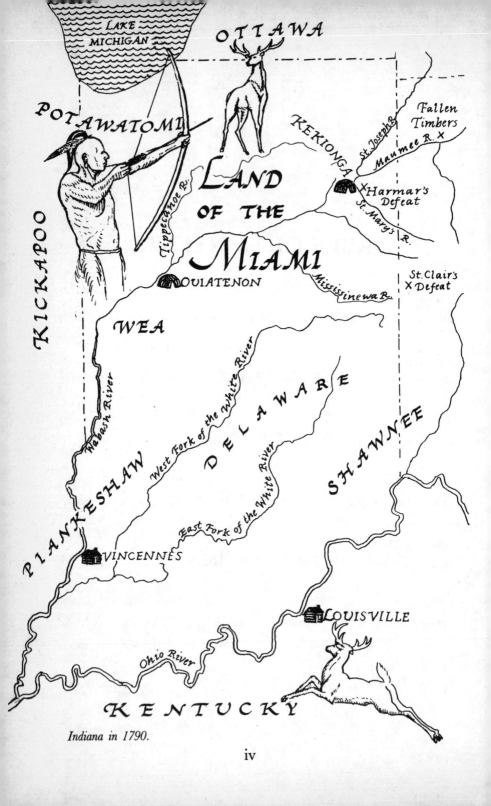

LAKE MICHIGAN

OTTAWA

POTAWATOMI

KICKAPOO

KEKIONGA

St. Joseph R.

Maumee R.

Fallen Timbers X

X Harmar's Defeat

St. Mary's R.

Tippecanoe R.

Land

of the

MIAMI

OUIATENON

Mississinewa R.

St. Clair's X Defeat

WEA

Wabash River

West Fork of the White River

D E L A W A R E

S H A W N E E

East Fork of the White River

P I A N K E S H A W

VINCENNES

LOUISVILLE

Ohio River

K E N T U C K Y

Indiana in 1790.

DEDICATION

This book is dedicated to the Miami Nation of Indians in Indiana and all the children who want to read about their ancestors.

The Battle of Tippecanoe from a drawing by Richard Day, now in Lewis Library, Vincennes, Indiana.

Chapter One

Introduction and Sa-kia's Tale

It is a dark night without stars. Smoke rises from a campfire burning bright with elm and oak logs. Around the fire sit tall men who have tattoos of snakes and turtles on their arms and chests. They smoke pipes of spicy herbs.

In front of them, women wearing heavy fringed skirts circle the fire dancing. And near the woods, behind them all, a priest wearing the head of a fox on his own head chants to drum and flute. The Miami Indians are celebrating the harvest festival.

The sacred, or Meda, priest leans over to a group of children playing in the edge of the woods. The children are making a noisy ring around a Frenchman who has just arrived to visit the camp. "Be quiet," the priest says. "The spirits of the woods do not like your noise. Let us all tell stories about our Miami people. Let our friend sit down and listen. Perhaps that will quiet you and the spirits of the woods will not be angry." The priest prepares the children to tell stories as the fire leaps and the harvest drum beats.

This scene could have happened in many villages in Indiana and Ohio just before the time of George Washington. The Miami Indians have gone now from the lakes and rivers. But for two hundred years or more they ruled the state where we live. They were the strongest, most feared tribe in America. They paddled their dugout canoes, they built their wigwams. They fought the battles to save their land on the very spots we live now. They had power, they told great tales, they lived as friends of animals, plants and all nature. Now they are gone. And we remember them with a sense of mystery.

Indians of long ago are always mysterious and interesting. The Miamis were that way too. One reason is that we do not know where they came from and how they got into Indiana and Ohio.

The old tales they told spoke of the "ancient ones." These Indian ancestors farmed and fished somewhere around the Mississippi and Ohio Rivers in days long ago, they said. Perhaps the Miamis' ancestors were part of the group of prehistoric Indians who lived in Indiana and Ohio and buried their dead in great tall hills.

Nobody knows what happened to the people who built the mounds, but they went away. When we finally first hear about the tribe called Miamis, they are the ones the pioneers knew. They were what we call woodland Indians. They hunted and fished and lived in bark and wood houses. They spoke a language like the Ot-ta-was and O-jib-was in Michigan, and the modern Pe-o-ri-as from Illinois.

But the Miamis were different from the other woodland Indians. Their religion, at least in early times, may have had sun worship in it. Nobody else around here had that tradition. Indians in Mexico and our South worshipped the sun. The Miamis had fine white corn to eat and make into meal. The other tribes had yellow corn. The other tribes loved to hunt best. The Miamis liked to farm as well as hunt, and they did it well.

And so the mysteries remain. Were the Miamis here in prehistoric times? Were the Miamis' ancestors the people who built the big burial mounds you sometimes see by the roads in Indiana and Ohio? If so, what made them leave those states? Did the Miamis learn to grow white corn in the far south from Indians there? If they did, what made them leave and come back here? Nobody knows. It is a mystery.

The first people to come across the Miamis in modern times were white traders who came to Wisconsin, Indiana, Illinois and Ohio in the 1600's The 1600's was the same time when the Pilgrims were living in America. The Midwest was still a wilderness.

The traders who first saw the Indians were from France. They were looking for mink and beaver furs to send to England and France to make fancy fur coats and hats.

The Indians hunted these animals and traded them to the French. The fur traders came in the spring in long canoes through the Great Lakes area. They had their boats full of trade goods. They brought pots, pans, beads of glass and metal tools. They also had wool cloth, tools, guns and bracelets and necklaces.

3

The traders began to write letters home about the Indians they saw. These Indians called themselves "We-miamiki," which meant "Beaver People" in the O-jib-wa Indian language. Perhaps other Indian tribes called the Miamis "beaver people" because the Miamis were very good at hunting the beavers which built their dams all over the rivers.

Sometimes English traders came too. They called the Miamis another name—the "Twightwees." They said that's what the Miamis called themselves sometimes. One trader wrote "This name Twightwees may come from the call of a bird these Indians love, the Red-winged blackbird who says 'twee tweee.' Or it may be from the call of the crane who says 'twa twa twa.' "

The Miamis may have been among the first tribes in Indiana, but during and after the Revolutionary War, there were other tribes in the state. Del-a-wares had camped on White River. Kick-a-poos were in and near Illinois. Shawnees were down by the Ohio, Pot-a-wa-to-mis were along the lakes in the South Bend area. Sometimes the Miamis fought with these other tribes. Often they got along as brothers and even found husbands and wives from among the other tribes.

The Miamis were divided into bands. Some called the Weas were over by the Wabash, by what is now Lafayette, Indiana. A group called the Pi-an-ke-shaws were by Vincennes and in southern Indiana. Some Miamis were along the northern Eel River and many were around rivers and lakes near what is now Fort Wayne.

The Fort Wayne band was the most important of all. They lived in a string of villages near the big one called Ke-ki-on-ga. It was right near where downtown Fort Wayne is today. Ke-ki-on-ga may mean "the place of clipped hair." Indians cut their hair before they went into battle, and Ke-ki-on-ga was sometimes a spot of battle. Some Miami bands were in Ohio too.

4

Miami land was a beautiful paradise. Pike fish six feet long swam in the rivers. Flocks of birds flew so thick they made the whole sky dark. Trees were as tall as skyscrapers, because they had grown for hundreds of years with no one to cut them.

Several thousand Indians lived among these beautiful woodlands. The Miamis were one of the bigger tribes.

All of these woodland Indians shared some of the same customs. They all lived in wigwams. These were round, cozy huts made of bent branches from trees covered with bark or mats. Indians in Indiana and Ohio did not live in tepees. Indians in the West, in states like Kansas, made tepees because they did not have wood to build fine huts. They had to build tents out of animal skins instead.

Woodland Indians did not ride on ponies like the Indians out west. Sometimes the white men traded them horses and they did use them for long distances. But usually the woodland Indians walked. They went on trails they blazed themselves by cutting slits in trees. They used the rivers and lakes, too, as roads, paddling with dugout canoes. Their life was simple and they felt happy in their woodland homes planting and growing corn, hunting game and trading furs to the few white people who came, and who were friendly to them.

War was an important part of Miami life at all times. The Miamis fought with other tribes before the white man came. The wars were over the right to hunt on certain lands. Later they fought hard with settlers when the white pioneers began to come into the Middle West, into Indiana and Ohio to farm.

But what they liked just as well as war was to live in peace as close family groups. Mother, father, sister, brothers, grandparents and aunts and uncles, gathering together in the wigwam in winter, telling tales of the river spirits as the wild wind blew outside. Or in summer, barefooted on the warm earth, scratching the land with little hoes and putting in seeds and water. Then watching the spears of corn grow, shoot tall and tassel. Finally, gathering the good grain to

5

make into flatcakes and cook with deer meat. Just as we do they enjoyed their work and their games, ceremonies and events that made up the Indian year.

Though they seem mysterious, they really weren't. The Miamis and all Indians were often wise, honest human beings who cared about the same things we do. As people they were the same as we. It was their ways that were fascinating and different—these Beaver People, these We-miamiki of the northern Midwest.

Now let us go back to our scene.

The logs on the campfire flame up. The smoke rises to the sky. The children sit down, their legs crossed in front of them and the Meda priest points to one of them to begin the tales. It is a girl of about eleven, who looks up at him with large, serious eyes and nods her head. The legend lives on. Let the tale begin.

I am Sa-kia, Crane girl, of the Miamis. I am daughter of the band chief here. I was born in the birth hut by the edge of the stream. My mother and two old women helped me into the world. Then the old grandmothers wrapped me in the skin of a doe, a baby deerskin. My diapers were pouches of deerskin filled with milkweed and cattail fluff.

I stayed always by my mother on the cradle board. She put this board to carry babies on her back. Or, if she was hoeing in the fields, which is the job of women, she could set it beside her. Sometimes it hung from a limb of a tree and my young cousins swung it, rocking me gently to sleep.

When I grew old enough to crawl about and walk, I went in and out of the summer hut which I loved. It was open to the air and covered with elm bark.

I did not cry very much. No Miami cries, even when he or she is little. Our mothers hush us. We dare not cry or our ene-

Tanning deer skins was a part of every Miami girl's life. Behind her is drying jerky or dried beef.

mies may hear and know where we are. And the warrior men do not like crying children. I know to keep quiet when the men are come back from battle, tired and hungry. Then my mother takes food from the pot and gives them the first dish. Children must stay at the back of the hut and they eat last of all.

All Miami girls learn to be strong wives and mothers. We do the important camp and home work of the tribe. The Great Spirit has made laws about men and women. The men fight the battles and get the game animals we eat to live on. The women build the summer and winter huts, tend the fields, and cook. They take care of children.

I do love to cook, to smell the fragrant wild onions when I cut them into the pot to stew with deer meat. I put in squash pieces and salt and let it simmer gently. At the end, just before I serve it up (to the men of course) I add corn meal to thicken it. If there is garlic, I can put this in. Chicago, that is our word for garlic. Some people say there is a place in the land of the Illinois where much of this grows and they call this place Chicago.

I cook all the things we grow and gather. There are pumpkins with maple sugar on them baked in the coals. There are the small nut-like tomatoes. We love these tomatoes. The white man says they are poisonous and will not eat them. I laugh at that! I have not died yet. Best of all I love the persimmons, picked when frost is come to the fields. With plenty of good maple sugar and meal, cooked in a pan in the coals, it is a good dish. When I serve persimmon pudding, even my father says I am a good cook.

How often I thank the Corn Spirit for this corn, this wonderful plant the "ancient ones" learned to use. The festival of the corn is good fun is it not? We have husked the ears and shelled them as a tribe now and we will put the grains in the clay corn pots.

These pots go in the winter holes lined with bark in the ground. They are put in secret places so if our enemies come into camp, they cannot find our food and destroy it.

We will take the corn out a little at a time. We can grind it into meal with the grinding bowl and stick. We can fry it on hot stones into cakes. We can cook it with molasses for the men to eat on the trail as a snack.

And the beans. Mixed with the corn and cooked with deer meat or eaten green in summer. How good they are!

What meats do we Miamis eat? I have heard the Meda priest say the chant.

> "Of the beasts of land you eat
> Elk, deer, bear and bison meat
> Panther and porcupine are sweet
> Of the water fowl in the lake
> Duck and goose and bittern take
> Heron and loon bad tastes will make."

8

Indians decorated their moccasins with porcupine quills.

Some people think we eat dogs. How silly. The O-jib-was in Michigan do this. Maybe they do not have other food. But I could never touch a camp pet. My brother used to laugh and remember a feast where the Miamis ate dog's head. Ugh.

Since the French have come, we have more work, both men and women. Boys and men go into the woods to kill the minks and beavers. Sometimes they are gone for weeks in winter. Women and girls tan the furs when they come back in. I am learning to do this well.

It is wonderfully exciting to see the men come in from a big kill in the woods, deer tied by their legs upside down and hanging from poles two men carry. Or if, as happens sometimes, there is a buffalo, big hairy bodies dragging behind a horse on a sledge.

Perhaps my father is one of the men whose arrow has wounded the buffalo or deer. Many arrows have gone from quivers into the animal. But only one would have killed him.

The hunter who claims the kill has the right to the best pieces of meat. If it is a buffalo, that will be the juicy, tender hump. If it is a bear, it will be the feet. After the hunter has taken his pick for his own family, the rest of the meat goes to all the members of the tribe. We share all, for has not the Great Spirit given all of Mother Earth's good things to all her children?

When the hunters are done cutting up the meat, we women come in. What a lot there is to do to prepare the hides! Buffalo hides make wonderful robes.

What would we do without the skins of our friends the animals! I love to snuggle down on a cold night on my bed in the winter house. It has poles bound together for me to lie on and they are hard and bumpy. But with a soft, warm animal skin to wrap up in, I sleep on a cloud. You can make deerskins into coats or pants or hang them up along the inside walls of the winter shelter to keep out the cold winds.

Buffalo hair looks shaggy and rough but a bison's hair can be used too, to weave, to make leggings and mittens. But first we must get the hair off the hide. My mother and aunts work with me on the robes we make. We take ashes from the fireplace and mix them with water in a big iron pot the white man has sold us. The ashes and water soak the long hair from the hide. It pulls out easily.

Then we must take our animal bone-scrapers and clean the hide. Blood and fat must come off the inner side. We lay the hide on a split log and scrape it hard.

But the next big thing is to get the skin soft. Hide leather, either deer or buffalo, will get very hard and crack if it is not treated. We call this tanning.

The way my aunts taught me to tan hides is this. You take the brains of the animals and crush them up. This is messy. And it smells awful, but it works. You soak the hide

10

in this brain oil, which has something in it that softens hides, and heat it up a little. Sometimes you can add bark of trees to the water in the pot where you soak the hides.

After the brains are rubbed into it, the hide is stretched and rubbed back and forth over a rope to soften it. When the hide is cooled it is so supple. After it is tanned, we must make it tough and water-proofed. It must be put on a stretching frame and held over a smoky fire. This part is awful, I tell you, although my mother says a Miami does not complain. The smoke hurts your eyes. Sometimes the old women cannot see. They have had their eyes too long in the smoke.

Buffalo and deer skins are not the only ones we must take care of. The beaver is worth much money when the trader comes. After we tan the back of his hide, we put the whole skin, with the hair on, on a beaver frame. A beaver frame is shaped like an egg. We stand it against a tree to dry in the right shape. There are also shapes for ermine, fisher and even bear. Some of the white men want bear coats! What will they think of next!

It is easier to make clothing out of the wool the trader brings. Many times we buy it raw and must dye it ourselves. I gather walnut to make a deep brown dye that we boil in a pot. First, though, my sisters and I must all stomp on the wool as it sits in the stream to shrink it up. We can make red from vermilion and yellow from tree of heaven.

What a good day it is when the trader comes. I love to go to the trader's canoe and watch my father pick out goods to exchange for the furs we have prepared. He looks carefully to be sure the axes that the trader bring are sharp and made of good steel. My mother wants kettles to fix venison stew and pans to fry rabbit in. And I want those lovely little crosses on chains. Double crosses they are, made of silver. My father says the silver is partly tin, but I don't care. My friends Bright Breeze and Loon Feather got double crosses on the last trip the trader made, and I waited all winter to get mine.

11

My mother, my friends and all the women love the bright beads the traders bring. We can sew them onto our clothes and the shirts the men wear.

Mother says I must be able to do very good quill work. I try, but my fingers are clumsy. My grandmother Owl Fright does good quill work. She takes the porcupine quills and bends them and makes wonderful flowers, hawks and pine trees which decorate our purses and baskets.

Soon it will be time to take up woman's duties. I will do the sacred things the people of my tribe have always done when they are ready to become women. These are the "becoming a woman" ceremonies.

My brother is going far into the wood to have his "moon-in-the-wild," when he will prove he is ready to be a man. I will have my vision time too, but I will not go so far into the woods.

Here is how I will do it. I will go out away from the camp. I will go for three days, perhaps. I will not eat. I will try not to sleep. Finally, after one or two days, I will be able to stand it no longer. I will fall asleep by a bubbling stream, lying on a bed of moss.

A vision will come to me, and it will tell me what I will do later in my life. My sacred favorite animal will come to me in a dream and tell me things. Bright Breeze had a hawk, greatest of all birds, come to her, and tell her that she would someday marry a white man. She could hardly walk when she got back and they had to give her drinks of water.

I will wait, ready for my vision. Perhaps a giant ma-qua, a bear, will come to me, standing on his hind legs. I will not be scared because I will know he is a dream. Will I be a great maker of cloth? A great quill woman? Will I marry the band chief's son of the Wea people? Or even a Shawnee? Who can say. The vision animal will tell me.

He will be with me all my life. I may not see him, but he will be there. He will guide me, help me if I get in trouble. And he will be my special prayer voice to the Great Spirit,

Ki-tchi-man-it-o-wac. He can ask for special things for me and my husband and my children.

Truly, I can hardly wait for my time of becoming a woman and going on my vision quest.

Then, when I am older, perhaps twenty, I will begin to dress very well. I will trim my hair and bathe in the stream even in the fall and spring. I will bring flowers into the wigwam. The man who will be my husband will be looking at me. He will be seeing if I am to be a good wife.

Of course, he will have to let me know he cares for me. He will do that the way all Miami young men do. He will come into my parents' home and lie down beside me on the ground in early evening. If I like him, I can turn to him and smile. Then he will leave. We will be promised to each other.

If I do not want him as a husband or have another I love, I will turn my back and he will feel bad and go away. Maybe then he will try other things. He may come to my parents and ask them to talk to me. He may bring lots of presents, not to buy me, but to please me and my parents. Maybe I will give in and marry him.

If I do, he will take me by the hand on the day of marrying. We will stand together before the tribe and band chief. Many presents will be given on both sides. Then we will be husband and wife and live in our own wigwam.

It will be good to be married. My husband and I will eat from the same bowl. For the first time I will eat from the bowl a man has touched.

I sometimes wonder why we women may not touch the men's sacred things. They say we are bad luck. We many not touch pipes they smoke, war tomahawks or bows and arrows or the sacred medicine pouch they carry to help them pray to the gods or Manittos.

And so, someday I shall have children too. They will go onto the cradle board and run among the cattails and play the children's games. But what will they grow up to? I worry. Already the white men come among us, as you do, trader. Some are moving into what they call Kentucky. Kentucky is the Dark and Bloody Ground where our people have always gone to hunt.

No one lives there, in Kentucky now. Long ago there was a great battle, so they say, between Indians of north and south, and no Indians will go there to live. They go to hunt the great herds of buffalo. These herds are so large that if you stand and watch as they pass along the path you can watch for two of your hours and not see the last one yet.

Now the white man has come into these hunting grounds. He takes our food and drives away the game. These white men build forts and plant crops and do not like the Indians. And some say soon they will come into these lands where we live.

Will we live as before? Will the deer run and prance beside the stream and the beaver and his babies build their pretty dams on the river I love? Will the pots be full and my children eat their deer meat in peace?

I hear my father whisper with the warriors. He says they will go to Kentucky and attack a fort there. There were raids like this in other years. There was killing and many brave warriors did not return. One of them was my oldest brother.

We must drive the white men out, my father says. These are our lands, he says. I must be a brave and strong Miami woman. I must sing the song of sadness for the dead ones and know that the fallen ones now ride the winds as warriors in the skies.

But sometimes, when I hear the winds howl in the great storms I think, as the priest tells us, it is our warriors. They are lonely and come back to ride the hills near their homes. And I hear my brother's cries on the wind and I sob. Yes, with my head down into the buffalo robe so no one will hear, I cry.

A giant ma-qua or bear appears in a vision to A-son-da-ki.

Chapter Two
A-son-da-ki's Tale: A Miami Boy

The women's dance is over and the men have begun to move in a chanting circle. Young girls who are fire-feeders are throwing huge sycamore logs on the fire. It blazes, sending sparks as far as the group listening to the stories.

A boy whose long legs are growing too fast for his leggings stands up. He looks without blinking at the French trader. He is an odd-looking Indian. He has red, almost curly hair. His face looks as dark as the others in the circle, and yet on it is the start of a beard. Indians do not have beards. He stands thinking for a moment before beginning.

You Frenchmen come often to the camp these days. You bring your priests to teach us how to worship God and you stay and take our furs. Then you marry our Indian women. This is all well and good. Now there are mixed blood Indians among us, your children. There is Richardville, Pesh-e-wa, the Wildcat. He says his father was a French nobleman and he is related through his mother to our highest chiefs.

The Miamis like you French. You have been good to us and treat us mostly as men, not dogs, as do the Americans. Of course you get a penny in your pocket for being good to us, too.

16

Your children, half-French, half-Miami will be welcomed among the Miami. I think it will ever be so.

As for the English, we have tried to like them. My own grandfather, Band Chief Rising Star, was a friend of the English at the time of what you call the French and Indian War.

There was a Miami village in the middle part of Ohio country. My grandfather and his brothers were there trading with English at Pickawillany, as they called it. The French got jealous and started a war. Many of my grandfather's relatives were killed by the French and other Indians. We fled north in Ohio country.

My mother's name is M'Tak-wa-pi-min-ji, Mulberry Blossom. You see her sitting there beside the smaller children. She was a very young maiden when she met my father, an American settler. He left her before I was born. As I came into the world, my mother looked out the door of the hut and saw the sun rising. She named me A-son-da-ki Ca-ip-awa, Shining Morning Sun.

My Uncle has been my best friend since I was a baby. Hidden Panther, Ki-no-za-wia. Now all Miamis call older men "Uncle" but this really is my uncle and a good one he is, too. He is away now at a council with Pi-an-ke-shaws in the south.

We lived in Ohio for a while. Then we came back to this Ke-ki-on-ga land. My uncle began to train me to be a Miami youth. Shall I tell you how he did it?

Imagine a morning in mid-summer. It is a beautiful morning. We are at the Lake of the Boulders, Lake Mock-sin-kic-kee west of Ke-ki-on-ga. My uncle has brought me to a forest schoolroom. You white men have schoolrooms inside cabins. Our Miami school is out-of-doors.

I have already learned the lesson of the months, so I can say them and what we Miami do in them by heart. If you do not know, trader, I will tell you.

17

We start with what you call March, Ma-kon-sa Moon. It is the month of the young bear.

Then there is April, An-da-kwa, Moon of the crow.

Next is May, Tca-tca-qua Moon, the Sand Hill Crane's time.

And June, Wi-ko-wi, whip-poor-will's moon.

Then July, Pap-sa-ka-wi-pin-wi-ki, Midsummer time

And August, Ki-cin-gwi-a, Green Corn time.

September, Mi-ci-wi-a, Elk's moon

October, Ca-ca-ka-yol-ia Moon, which means grass burns in streaks.

November, Ki-ol-i-a Moon, smoky burning time.

December, Ai-a-pan-sa, young buck moon.

January Ai-a-pi-a, full-grown buck time.

February, Ma-qua, Bear Moon.

Those are the Miami moons. Are they not more interesting than yours?

My uncle had brought me to a summer fishing camp above the round lake. Often we sat and watched the still water glimmer below us and talked about being We-miamiki, one of the people.

"We are a people of the woods," my uncle said. And he taught me the skills of the trail. How to bend trees at right angles to show others which way to go, how to make signs on big rocks. And then how to watch a raccoon's tracks to see how hard the mud around them was to tell how long since he had been past.

"A good hunter will walk in the dew of the morning to mask his footsteps. One getting away from an enemy will walk only on rock or in the water if he can. Hide your smell with the oil of bear or with crushed mint. And carry the right weapon. He who goes to meet the bear with only a twig meets his death instead." That is what my uncle said.

I had many questions. "Is that a blue racer, Uncle?" I asked. I was watching a snake slither through the bog.

18

March   April   May

June   July   August

These are the months of the Indian year.

September   October   November

December   January   February

"No, that is the father of all the snakes, the black snake. He is the smartest of all those who go on the belly. He can climb trees. Blue racer makes us scared but he is not deadly. But stay aware from Ci-ci-kwia with rattles and spots."

"Yes," I said. "He brings death in his fangs. And he is sacred. He puts off his skin when it is the time to plant corn. I will watch for him."

Sometimes we sat in a canoe on Lake Mock-sin-kic-kee. We had made the canoe ourselves. We took a log and chopped a little bit out and made a fire in it. Soon there were coals. We kept adding more coals. We blew on the fire in the tree with po-to-ta-kini, fire blow pipe. At last the tree burned itself out and was hollow and it was our boat.

At times my uncle and I sat together for hours. We listened to the silly call of the loon, laughing. We saw how pebbles in the water make ripples like designs on Ir-o-quois belts.

"We are a people of the water," My uncle would say. "Once, before the white man came we were lords of all the land from the large lake west to the Grandfather River south to Beautiful Ohio waters.

"So we know the waters well. You must be able to see the proud ways of Sa-kia the heron. You must make friends with Ko-ka the frog.

"There are different kinds of ducks, maybe twenty. You must be able to tell a canvas-back from a mallard duck."

He taught me to make fire, to use rawhide, to shoot straight. We took mulberry and ash sticks and bent them to make fine bows. We made arrows with good French steel for tips. Some old people still use the flint tips from the flint pits, which we ride far to get. But we use new steel.

What Uncle was getting me ready for was the Moon-in-the-wild. It was going to be my manhood trip into the woods. Soon I would go alone for a month, with only a knife. I must survive, by myself. The things he had taught me would mean whether I would live or die.

20

George Winter's Indian camp scene (used with permission of the Tippecanoe County Historical Society).

When I thought about the Moon-in-the-wild, sometimes I wanted it to come. Sometimes I did not. I could not tell my uncle what sometimes I thought about in the night, when my mother slept. I worried because I was not very brave. Perhaps it was because I was half-American, but I seemed to feel pain easier than my Indian cousins.

And once we went far away into the country of the Illinois. We hunted and the buffalo came crashing down, their horns sharp and their heads low. I wanted to scream and run. It was all I could do to keep my place behind the safe tree where my uncle had placed me.

Now that I was in the wild on my moon, what I really wanted to do was prove myself as a real Miami. I wanted to be named We-miamiki, member of the people of my tribe. I especially wanted to show the chief, Little Turtle, who I was, make him notice me. I knew that because I was half-American, he did not much like me, and the rest of the tribe felt the same.

Had he noticed I was not brave? There was something in his eyes once when he saw me watch the tormenting of a white captive.

I did not like this torturing. It is our people's way to test our captives, to see if they are men. Sometimes even the women do cruel things to see if they will cry out. It is our way and I know it. Brave ones will live and get adopted into the tribe. Cowards will die.

Sometimes the deaths are horrible. In past times we burned captives at the stake. Now we put fire sticks in their skin. But I feel sick when this happens, and I know that if I were being poked at with hot fire, I would be afraid. Maybe even scream. I think Little Turtle knew it.

Perhaps it is not that at all. Maybe he just hates me because he hates all Americans. All Miamis do. After all, who could blame them. The Americans are pushing their nosy noses into every part of our land, killing the game, scaring the animals away.

They play their silly fiddles, shoot their fire sticks, guns, and wrinkle up their faces at us. They say we smell. They act as if we are stupid.

We Indians, who can walk without making a sound, whose minds and hearts can understand the language of the deer and bear. They think we are stupid.

Even though I am half white, I do not understand the white man. They came long ago far away from here, to a place called Massachusetts. English pilgrims. They said they wanted only a little land, only a piece. We Indians gave them some, after all, had not the Great Spirit given to all? Then they wanted more, always more.

They made our Del-a-ware brothers put scratches on pieces of paper to give them more land. In return we were to be left in peace to hunt and fish in the woods that were left. But there they came again. White men are like dogs that

22

Little Turtle, the great Miami chief, was given a medal by George Washington after he visited the capitol. From a portrait by Gilbert Stuart.

follow you all about. You cannot hide. Go over the mountains, they come running after you. Cross the Great Lakes, they are standing waiting for you on the shore. Where can we go? What can we do?

Perhaps that is why Little Turtle hates them so. Some people say Little Turtle, Me-she-kin-o-qua, is the greatest chief the Indians have ever had. He talks to the white man with wisdom. He leads the Indians with bravery. And now he is saying that the white man can never have this land, that the Miamis will lead all tribes to claim their birth right.

And so, I was going to prove to Little Turtle, the great chief, that I was worthy of being We-miamiki, a Miami man. I was to have my Moon-in-the-wild.

Little Turtle saw me off on that day in Spring and I could not read what was in his eyes. All he said was "A lam sang kati"—there will be strong wind.

Let me take you to that time two years ago.

I went north into the woods, miles from Ke-ki-on-ga. Its villages of Miami, and now Del-a-ware and Shaw-nee tribes. too, seemed far away. I could only think this: it is May and I am in the woods alone. Squirrels flashed their high tails at me. Bees buzzed. Birds sang above white violets.

Well, the first thing I would need, I told myself, was shelter. Good, my uncle had taught me how to build a lean-to. Take branches off of trees, make forks in two of the best, stick them in the ground. Put a cross stick between them. Then place other branches against it to make a slanting roof. Get some pine branches and put them on the floor. That makes a good shelter.

The first day it rained hard and I stayed inside. A fine thing, I thought. Here I am at my big time and it rains and blows. But I had seen a good sign when I woke up that day. A big spider had made a web by a tree outside my lean-to. Perhaps that spider, as the Miamis believe, was the spirit of my Grandmother watching over me. That would be good. I needed somebody. I was getting very hungry.

I dug some wild parsley root and ate it. There were no berries yet, but I found some nuts left over from last year under a tree and ate them. Then I went to catch fish in the stream. I made a barrier at a narrow part of the stream and with my knife I whittled a strong spear. When they came by, there! I speared a good big river carp.

I cleaned him with my knife. It was the only thing I could take with me. It was too much trouble to cook the fish. I popped open some mussels. Raw fish and raw mussels. I had the best dinner of my life. Hunger is the best thing you can add to food, the Indians say.

And so I settled in for several days in a row of good weather, fishing, digging roots and resting. A Moon-in-the-wild is not so hard, I told myself. I had found a dead deer by the creek the third day out. I was able to skin and scrape it enough to use the hide to keep me warm when I needed it.

I was even getting used to having almost no clothes on. My people have always been proud that they are tough. Even in the coldest weather Miamis wear only shirt, leggings, blanket and moccasins.

My uncle said if my feet were warm and dry I would feel warm too. He made my feet tough by making me walk around with salt in my moccasins. Now I can step on rocks, sticks, even a small thorn and not feel it.

But after a few days I wanted real meat. I knew it was time to set a snare. I crushed up catnip leaves to mask my scent a little and went to a meadow where I had seen rabbits at play. Sure enough, there they were in the early morning sunlight, nibbling and talking to their friends.

With a rock I dug a cattail root. Rabbits love cattail root. It does have a good, nutty flavor like the potatoes you white men love so much. I bent over a little tree to make a trigger for my trap, just as my uncle had taught me.

I tied the top down with some sinew from the dead deer. Sinew is like your twine; I had wound a big ball of it.

I broke off another little tree and fixed it as a stake in the ground. This made a little circle, a little lasso, with the bait hidden inside it. The rabbit would come up, nibble at the root, and the loop would tighten and fling him in the air. He would be my supper!

I would have to wait about three hours for my scent to leave this clearing. I waited. I had no patience. My mouth was watering at the thought of roasted rabbit!

And, when I went back to the clearing a fat brown rabbit was in the snare. "The spirits, the Manittos, are good," I shouted to nobody. I danced around the clearing. "I am a hunter on my own. I will be named We-miamiki when I return."

Now I must skin and cook the catch. The skinning I did in three minutes with a very sharp stone. Now I would make my first fire in the wild. I gathered tinder. Then I found fluff from an old hornet's nest. I picked up some of last fall's leaves and two sticks just the right size.

They had to feel just right to rub together. Rub, rub, do not let the wrists feel tired, be ready to toss the tinder fluff in the air and blow at the first spark you get off the sticks.

I worked for three minutes. No spark. I rested. Then I tried again. This time the spark flew off. But the tinder did not catch fire. I was getting angry. Bugs flew and hummed in my ears. They landed on my eyes and lips. I hated this old-fashioned way of making fire. The fire stick with a pointy shaft and bowstring is much better at making sparks.

I said a prayer to the Manittos, the spirits that are in all things. "Just a little glow is all I need, Manittos. It will catch and get bigger."

Then I took out a little bit of fine fluff, cotton and milk-weed that I had stored in a secret place—my belly button. I kept thinking of Little Turtle. I prayed one more time "We-miamiki let it light." I rubbed, struck and a small glow came onto the fine lint. I blew with just the right amount of breath. The fire started. I moved it to a second pile of dry cottonwood and the smallest of twigs. "Thank you, Manittos," I breathed.

And so I got through almost the whole month. I was learning so many lessons about becoming We-miamiki, Miami man. Sometimes I talked to myself out there and this is what I said.

"Being We-miamiki means walking in the moccasins of the Great Spirit as he looks at animals. We must think as the owl thinks. Know the raccoon's tricks. And how the deer heads to water when he is wounded.

"And we must love all creation as the Great Spirit loves and not be mad at the bee when he stings us." This I said as

I put some mud and moss on a place where a bee had stung me.

"We-miamiki do not waste as the white man wastes," I said to myself. "We use only what is needed." This I said as I put back the moss I did not need after I used some on the sting.

I remembered how Uncle had told me about the meaning of nature. He said all things need each other. "Long ago in the skies there were a race of Great Beings. All lived in peace there. But the minds of some of the beings were changed and they were kicked out of the skies. Then a race of men had to be made on earth. A flood of water was on the earth. Out of a hole in the sky fell the Earth Mother. She landed on an island where animals came to her to help her. One of the first was the Great Hare, or Rabbit.

"The Earth Mother grew bigger and bigger and part of her went into every living thing. She gave her magic to all and each has its part. The beaver builds his dam, bees make honey. Man rules the earth and all the other animals. So all comes from Earth Mother and each has its own magic spirit. We must not hurt the magic spirit of a thing or animal. We must pray to them, the spirit helpers or Manittos in each thing. They can help us do what we need to do."

"Most of all, We-miamiki will be brave. He will not give in to pain and he will face death as a wildcat does, looking it in the eye," I said.

I had to think of that often on the last few days, because it was time for my vision quest and I was put to the test in ways I had never expected.

To get a vision quest, I had to stop eating and drinking, and sleeping. After three days, a dream would come to me. It was not easy but I did it. The first day I saw pots of cooking meat on the clouds and they called to me. The second day I could think of nothing but meat and corn. They danced before my eyes. But the third day hunger and thirst left me, and I finally slept.

27

When I awoke towards sunset I saw a giant bear in my dream, standing before me on my hind legs. The ma-qua spoke quietly and told me, "You will seek much and find little." I shrugged my shoulders. That did not mean much to me. The bear also told me there would be a great contest in the morning. I would earn my name at the contest. A new name! I would wait and pray and get ready to see what it would be.

When the sun rose, I went to eat. I was as hungry as a bear in Ma-kon-sa Moon after he has slept all winter. My head felt dizzy and somehow I didn't care about anything. I felt daring, like little boys who walk out on the ice a step at a time, daring it to fall through. Such a type of thinking is dangerous in the Moon-in-the-wild.

"I will make my own test," I thought. "I am a hunter on my own and my Moon-in-the-wild is almost over. I will do a great thing and build a bear pit."

Yes, my uncle had told me that I would not need to do this at all out in the wild. That it was done by a group of hunters who know bear. Yes, I knew the bear I would trap would be too large for me to carry home and I would have to get help and come back. Never mind. I wanted to do it. Perhaps it was to show off.

So, I dug a pit. It was in a place of peat moss, soft enough so I could scoop out the dirt but not so soft that water would come into my hole. For almost two days I dug with rocks, sticks and my own hands. It got so I could think of nothing else.

Finally the hole was six feet long and six feet high. As my uncle told me, I took a branch into the hole with me always as the hole got deep. I did that so I would have something to climb out on. I did not want to be the bear myself, trapped in my own hole.

I began to think of the real bear that might get in here. And I felt the old fear come in. I was not brave yet. I grumbled to myself not to mind.

28

Now I must bait the trap. What better bait than one of the rabbits I was so good at catching now. I made my snare, caught a small rabbit and then tied some of the deer rawhide around his stomach. The rawhide was wet. I knew that as it shrunk up, it would tighten around the rabbit's stomach. He would cry out. The bear would hear him and come and then—of course. Into the pit with the ma-qua.

I covered my trap with hemlock limbs and pranced about. My pride in myself was bigger than a hornet's nest. I had had my man's vision easily, not like some of the boys who had to go to the woods two or three times. I had fed myself, kept warm——and now a bear pit. What a man I was!

Suddenly I saw a half-dead oak in front of me with what seemed to be a cloud around its upper branches. It was a bee tree.

Why, I thought, it will be nothing for a man such as I to climb this bee tree and get some honey. I will do it while I wait for the bear. And so I raced over to the tree. I knew I must go up in this tree quickly and get the honey and get back down before the bees swarmed over me.

Up, up through branches I swung. I was floating on my new show-off pride as well as my arms. Now I could see the nest, an odd bumpy thing up there, with only a few bees about it. Ah, here it was. Soon I had my hands in the sweet, good stuff, jamming the honey and comb in my mouth at once. It came out of the hive. It spilled all over my legs and feet.

But what was this? The bees were back, more than I had thought, suddenly all over me. I must get down. I began to clamber down rapidly, my hands and feet sticky with honey, down down, swinging faster and faster as the bees buzzed, nipped, stung me.

Then there was a sense of slipping. I heard a crack. I felt myself fall a long, terrible moment. I bumped and scraped and came to a stop. I was in the fork of a tree and I was in terrible pain.

29

Miami canoes were dugouts made with fire coals.

I had done the thing no Indian alone must ever do. I had broken my leg. After I came to myself I wanted to pound on the tree, to scream. But I did not do it. I was more afraid than I had ever been in my life. All my pride was gone. I had not one shred of bravery left.

Yet the word came to me. We-miamiki. Being a man, a Miami man. I calmed myself. It was almost as if the tree had spoken to me.

I talked out loud and my voice was odd because my teeth were gritted. "Here is what you must do, We-miamiki. At least you did not hit the ground which could have killed you. The Manitto of the tree has saved your life."

And I answered myself. "You must lift yourself by your arms and one good leg down out of this tree, no matter what the pain. And then you know what you must do."

And so, some way I took myself mostly by my arms down out of that tree and onto the ground. I lay out of my head, almost, for an hour or so.

Then I made myself sit up and said to myself again, "Now, We-miamiki, you know what is next. You must pray and prepare for it."

Then I dragged myself, crawled and hopped, biting my lip to keep from crying out to the short stump of a tree.

I touched the ball of hide and sinew strips I had bound around my neck that morning. I reached to pick up two stout sticks. Soon I would need them.

I spoke to the tree. "Manitto, spirit of this tree, help me. I cannot live alone in the woods unless this leg is set. Drive out any evil spirit if one should be nearby and keep away the bear I may have called to that foolish pit. Crippled as I am, he could kill me now. And please send bravery to my spirit."

One last time I said the word "We-miamiki." The memory of all those good warriors back at the camp, always full of courage, gave me strength. I swung my leg onto the stump. When it was up there, I kicked it against the stump. I shrieked out in great pain. Then I sank slowly to the ground on my good leg. I knew no more for quite awhile. When I awoke I saw my broken leg still on the stump, bone pieces now set and rejoining.

Four days later, thin from having eaten nothing but hopping with a crutch, I came back into camp. My mother ran to comfort me. I pushed her back gently.

I went into the wigwam of Little Turtle. My uncle was there.

"So, the American boy has broken his leg on the Moon-in-the-wild," the chief said looking at me.

"True he has broken it. And true he has set it all alone," my uncle said. "Give him the tokens of manhood of the Miamis."

"Perhaps we will. But should we really?" Little Turtle turned away. "He is still half American. And wounded too.

31

From now on in we will call him A-son-da-ki A-la-me-lon-da. Wounded sun. That will be his new name."

One of my problems was that I sometimes blushed, and now I did it. I did not like my new name.

Still, the next week the tribe leaders gave me a medicine bag of deer leather filled with turkey feathers and beads to show I was now a man. But it was not what I expected. The feathers of a turkey, a fat, stupid bird are not the feathers of the noble hawk.

So the vision bear was right. I did look for something, and I did not get it.

But the bear was also wrong. I got something else. Out there in the woods I found my bravery. And that is the best prize of all, isn't it?

Fire-Tiger upset canoes in the Miss-is-sin-e-wa River.

33

Chapter Three

Minji's Tale: Folk Tales of the Miamis

The tale is long. Some of the little ones have fallen asleep, and their mothers come and pick them up to take them into the wigwams. The sky has cleared and a few clouds drift across the moon. "Tell us the tales of the West Wind," say the older children. "Minji, you know them best."

They turn to a lovely Indian woman whose hair is clasped with a pin on the back of her head. It is A-son-da-ki's mother.

The trader asks them to wait a moment while he fills his pipe. He puts in kinnick-i-nick herbs. They are good smelling weeds and plants instead of the tobacco that some of the Indians smoke.

When he lights the pipe, the woman begins.

"I am M'tak-wa-pi-min-ji but all here now call me Minji. I do not blame them, for my name is as long as the trail to Cherokee Land. I am the mother of that red-haired fox over there who just told the story. He is full of talk and perhaps I shall be too. You wish stories of the West Wind's child? Let me see . . .

NANAHBOOZHOO STEALS FIRE

Nan-ah-booz-hoo was the strongest, cleverest, best young man the earth has seen. He was a great god with magic at his beck and call. All Indian peoples know of him. Hi-a-wa-tha, some call him although he has many names. We call him Nan-ah-booz-hoo. He was hero to all the Indian peoples. His mother was Win-on-ah, his father the West Wind himself.

Why did he get to be such a hero? I will tell you. In the old, old days there were fewer people in the forests than now. They did not have as many comforts as they now have. Indeed, they missed something we think very important. They did not have fire, to cook and keep warm with. Sometimes they saw the lightning set fire to a particular tree and tried to keep some of the fire in the tree, but they did not seem to be able to keep it well. So they were often cold and ate raw food.

Nan-ah-booz-hoo was living at that time with No-ko-mis, his grandmother, the daughter of the moon. He was sorry to see that she was often so cold. Nan-ah-booz-hoo put his wits to work. What could he do to get some fire? He asked a coyote. "The fire is under the earth," said the coyote. There is a lot of it. Sometimes I go to the fire mountain, where it comes forth, and manage to snatch some from the bad Manittos who guard it."

"Who has it? Nan-ah-booz-hoo asked.

"A fierce warrior and his daughters. They are set up by the Manittos. They will not part with fire, because they think we on the earth are too stupid to have it. We will hurt ourselves and destroy all around us, they say."

"Has anyone except you, coyote, tried to get fire from the warrior and his daughters?"

"Many, my strong young friend. And they have all died."

For a moment Nan-ah-booz-hoo was afraid. And then he said, "Fire is a real friend to man. I will get it for all the Indian peoples."

Nan-ah-booz-hoo took his canoe and put it into the river. He paddled east as far as he could go. It was very cold by now and ice was beginning to form. Nan-ah-booz-hoo beached his canoe. Now, Nan-ah-booz-hoo the hero is also a trickster. He thought he would take on a disguise. He turned himself into a rabbit. He knew that the two daughters would soon be coming to the river to get water for the cooking pots.

Sure enough, there they came. Nan-ah-booz-hoo the rabbit jumped into the edge of the water and got himself very cold and dripping wet. Then he started limping around in front of the two daughters of the fire keeper.

These girls took pity on the rabbit and picked him up to carry him to their warm wigwam. They set him down in front of the sacred fire so that he might get warm.

Seeing that he was so happy by the fire, the girls went their way. Their father, the keeper of the fire, was asleep in another part of the wigwam. Nan-ah-booz-hoo rabbit moved closer to the fire. He thought to himself that he could get the end of one of the bigger sticks. It was on fire and sticking out.

But as the little rabbit went towards the fire, the earth shook in anger. It was mad because he was trying to take fire.

The fire-keeper woke up and called for his daughters. "Is anything the matter, my daughters?" he asked.

"No, Father. All we have done is bring a poor shivering rabbit in to get out of the cold."

The fire-keeper took a look at Nan-ah-booz-hoo, but could see nothing to be afraid of. As soon as he was snoring again, Nan-ah-booz-hoo picked up the burning stick by the cool end. He quickly changed himself into a young Indian runner.

He ran from the wigwam with the stick, heading towards the canoe as fast as he could. The daughters were magic women. They knew the bad Manittos would punish them for letting Nan-ah-booz-hoo get the fire. "Stop!" they cried. "You will be punished for stealing this sacred fire."

He did not listen to them and ran even faster. Now only a dried-up meadow remained between him and the canoe. Suddenly he had an idea. He put the burning stick onto the dry grass in the meadow, touching it first here, then there. The wind was in his face, so the smoke and fire blew back towards the two magic women, daughters of the fire-keeper.

Nan-ah-booz-hoo thus got back to his canoe and pushed it off for home. He stuck the burning stick in the front of the canoe and got away. The trip was not easy. Ice was forming on the river. The burning stick kept sending its sparks and fire back onto him, burning his skin. But he kept on.

Finally he came to his home. No-ko-mis, his grandmother was there, anxiously waiting for him to return. She was happy to see him and took care of his burns. Naturally, she was happy for the fire. They called all the Indian peoples together and gave them some coals.

But the families were not good about keeping the fire going. Sometimes they let it go out and had to go next door and get some from a nearby wigwam. Nan-ah-booz-hoo worried about that. What if all the fires in the village went out at once? He did not think he could get it a second time from the fire-keeper and his daughters, who were now very angry at him.

"Now Indian people can have fire to keep warm," Nanahboozhoo cries as he steals it from the fire-keepers.

We went into the woods to pray. "Great Spirit," he said, "what can we do to keep the fire that is so helpful to us all?"

The Great Spirit told him how fire was made. He showed him that sticks could be rubbed together till the friction made a spark. He told him how a bow string wound around a pointed stick and rubbed back and forth could strike sparks. He also showed him how you could strike together flint and a piece of iron and make the sparks fly into soft stuff. Then, blowing, you could get a fire to go. Nan-ah-booz-hoo went happily home. Now the Indian peoples could always have fire, even if it went out at their campfires.

HOW FIRE FIRST CAME OUT OF THE EARTH

"Tell us how that fire-keeper got the fire in the first place!" the children in the clearing shouted. Minji raised her

hand to quiet them and smiled. She nodded. After all, the evening was young still.

All right. I will tell you that story. I heard it from my father Rising Star. He took a trip once to the western mountains, far away, across the lands of the pony-riding Indians. Near the mountains, an old story-teller told him this:

Long ago there was not much need for fire. The earth was much warmer than it is now. Fruits, berries and delicious things grew everywhere for people to pick and eat as they would. Many strange animals were about, animals we do not now have. But then a disaster struck the earth. Things changed and the earth grew much colder. So the people did not have enough fruits and roots and needed to kill the animals and cook and eat them.

Fire was kept in the center of the earth by a magician named Sis-nin-i-koo. The Manittos kept it down there, far inside the caves of earth, because someone had told them if earth people got hold of fire they would not use it well and would destroy the earth. So they kept it hidden in the deep dark, way down inside the earth.

There were four doors into the hidden fire in the earth. At the first door was a great snake. At the second door was a mountain lion. Beyond that was a door with a great grizzly bear at its entrance. Beyond that, guarding the fire itself was Sis-nin-i-koo the magician.

The Indians were upset. They did not see how anyone could get past all those doors to get the fire.

But they decided to try anyway. They asked the fox to go down into the earth and try to get the fire. But he only got as far as the snake. The snake twined around his neck and almost ate him up before he got away. He ran to the Indians and said he would not try more.

"Who can we get?" the Indians asked themselves.

One smart Indian said that he had heard the coyote used to live under the ground and he knew his way around. "Hurry," the people told him. "It is getting colder." So the coyote agreed and began his trip to the inside of the earth.

There was a sort of cave which marked the entrance to the center of the earth, and the coyote headed towards it. Sure enough, the cold was getting worse on the face of the earth. There was ice over the mouth of the cave.

The coyote knew the habits of the animals. He waited until they had eaten and were asleep, then he crept past them. Sis-nin-i-koo the magician was also asleep. The coyote went up to the fire and with his teeth grabbed out a burning stick. But this woke up Sis-nin-i-koo.

"Someone has stolen fire," Sis-nin-i-koo shouted.

"Quickly, close your doors, keepers, before this coyote gets through." But the coyote made it through each door just before the bad beast snapped his jaws to eat him.

When the coyote brought the fire the Indians were glad to see it. But soon it got away and burned off a big part of the woods and the coyote decided to give it to the keeper and his two daughters. And that is how it came to where Nan-ah-booz-hoo found it and stole it so the Indians could keep it always.

NAN-AH-BOOZ-HOO AND THE BEES AND ROSES.

Nan-ah-booz-hoo was particularly kind to the small folk of Mother Earth, even to the mice and insects. One day he left his home on Spirit Lake and visited many parts of the river lands and the Great Lakes. At one spot he saw a sad group of bees. Even though my son A-son-da-ki A-la-me-lon-da got bitten by bees, it was not always so.

Once bees did not have stings. They made their beautiful honey and all the world could take it. And they did. The bears put their paws in it. Birds with long beaks stole it. And the busy bees died of hunger.

The chipmunk felt sorry for men and brought healing herbs to help them.

"Oh, Son of the West Wind, Nan-ah-booz-hoo, help us. Give us something to keep these robbers from our door," the bees buzzed as they saw the hero.

West Wind's Son looked at them with kindness. "You give so freely to all of your honey. But you must be able to keep some of it for yourselves. From now on in you will have stingers to warn robbers to keep away and punish them if they take what is yours."

The bees said "Thank you" and went away with new stings. And to this day you can find out what those are if you go too close to their homes without permission.

WHY ROSES HAVE THORNS

The roses, hearing about the bees, began to think about their problem. "We try to be lovely. We smell sweet, we paint our petals with beautiful colors. Pink, red, orange—but what happens? Everybody comes and picks us."

They decided to go see Nan-ah-booz-hoo. Now he had a nice wigwam, and he had just made it even prettier by putting a hedge of roses all around it.

That very day, when he had come out, he had chanced to see many rabbits eating the roses, stems and all.

A group of roses came up to him. "Oh Spirit of Spirit Lake, we salute you."

"Yes, maidens, what do you want?" he asked, wishing they would get to the point.

"We are beautiful, are we not?"

"Who can deny that?" he said. What was it they wanted?

"Everyone picks us."

"They wish to take your beauty with them to their own wigwams."

"Help us. We do not wish to be picked. Let us grow where we are."

He looked at his own rose hedge and said, "From now on in you will have thorns. Then the thief who wishes to pluck your beauty will have to think twice. He may get his finger pricked. Perhaps then he will leave you alone."

The roses thanked him with tears in their eyes, and to this day they have thorns. Now they are not easy to pick and thus they are more often left alone.

HOW THE ANIMALS SENT SICKNESS TO MAN

"Tell us the story of the animals having a council," said several little girls, pulling on Minji's skirt.

"What? Will you never let my voice rest. Well, all right, one or two more stories."

Long ago the animals decided to have a meeting. The bear called all of them together and said, "These men are ruining us now that they have fire. They wish much delicious meat to

"I can't get this thing to shoot," says a bear trying to work a bow and arrow in the Indian myth.

cook. They are killing our relatives, our uncles and children for their cooking pots."

"It is true," said the birds. "They shoot us with bows and arrows and catch us in snares. Let us act against them. It is war."

So the animals tried to decide what they could do to stop men. "Let us shoot them with bows and arrows," said the wolf. "That is how they injure us." The animals nodded their beaks, snouts and muzzles. A bear who had been kept as a pet and had seen how bows and arrows were made, showed a dog how to make one. As soon as it was done, the bears lined up to try it out.

"Wait. I cannot get this thing to work," said a young bear. Other bears tried with the same luck.

"A bad Manitto is getting in the way. Our claws are too long."

"Why not cut them?" asked a deer.

"We need them to snare fish in the river and to grab our food in other ways."

"I have an idea," said the deer. "We will get even with them. We will send diseases to them."

"Yes," said the bear. "I will be in charge of aching bones. Every time one of them comes for me, if he doesn't apologize for trying to kill me, I will send rheumatism to him." And that is why all Indian warriors to this day apologize if they must kill a bear—they are afraid he'll send them a sickness.

All the animals had ideas. The mosquito said he would bite them and give them fevers. The birds said they would give them colds and coughs. Each animal had a different sickness he would send to man.

And that is how diseases got into the world. Now we must call the shaman, the medicine man, to rid us of these bad things. Perhaps if we had been kinder to the friends in the animal kingdom, we would not have disease today. And wouldn't that be good?

HOW MEDICINE CAME

Well, but the humans needed something to defend themselves after the animals brought disease into the world. Help did come, because the Indians had a friend among the animals. He was the chipmunk.

This little creature loved men, because they often made a pet of him. They fed him little bits of food from their meals and loved to chase and look at him. So he felt sad when he saw what sickness the people were having now in the world.

He went about to all the plants and trees, who were friendly to man. He told them about the animals, and what they had done to hurt man.

44

"We will help," said the trees. They held a council. All the trees spoke. The pine and spruce trees said they would give their sap to make gum to help wounds close up. The elm said it would give its bark to make a drink which would heal people's troubles. The sassafras said it would give its roots to make wonderful tea which will bring back health.

Catnip said it too could be made into tea. Peppermint and wild ginger and raspberry and foxglove all said they would help too. And so medicines came into being.

The chipmunk said a polite thank you to the plants and ran to tell the Indian men and women about the gifts the trees and flowers had given man.

And that is why you never see an Indian child hurt a chipmunk, and why the chipmunk stays near the homes of men.

It knows that man is its friend. All Indian children remember the old Father Chipmunk and his kindness to men. They would not hurt the chipmunk for the world.

A-son-da-ki Al-a-me-lon-da has jumped up from his seat near the Frenchman.

"My mother has told you tales of roses and bees," he says. Everyone is drowsy. The moon has gone back under a cloud. "Sweet stories. The good Son of the West Wind and why chipmunks stay by the winter shelters. Chipmunks indeed! These are women's tales. I will tell you men's tales. Tales to make your scalps tingle. Adventure tales!"

All the children and even the two men murmur happily. Everyone loves an adventure tale.

FIRE TIGER AND GREAT HARE

The tale of Earth Mother is not the only one of the creation of the world. Another one we know is that when the world was created there was all water and no dry land. On the water floated a raft with all the animals of the world.

The smartest and quickest was Great Hare, Mitch-a-boo. He told the animals that if someone could get some land they could get off the raft.

Beaver and Otter tried but couldn't. Muskrat got one grain of sand and Mitch-a-boo said that was enough. With his cleverness he could build an island. And he did. All the animals stayed there and little by little Mich-a-boo made man too.

But one animal didn't like Mitch-a-boo and that was Fire Tiger. Mi-ci-bi-si. He plotted to kill Great Hare and almost succeeded. Then he grew very bitter and became the enemy of the men the Great Hare had created.

How could he hurt them most, he asked. By staying under the waters where the Indian peoples lived. Scaring them. Turning over their canoes when they passed by. Reaching up LIKE THIS AND GRABBING THEM. Did I scare you, little one by grabbing you in the dark? I meant to. I feel scary tonight.

If you go to Mis-sis-sin-e-wa River and stay with our people there, you had better look out for Fire Cat. He lives under the rapids. When your canoe goes over, WHISH! You'll be in the water. Then a cat's paw will reach out from under the ripples and slowly, slowly, PULL YOU UNDER. You don't believe me, small one? Just look in the water sometime when you're going over the rapids. I dare you.

Fire Tiger has a human face. He glares at you out of the water. If you see him, you'll have bad luck that day. But you can't get away from Mi-ci-bi-si even if you stay away from the water. Why? Because he can go anywhere on earth he wants. And the other place he goes is in the sky.

Yes, up there where he can see us all. Have you ever seen a ball in the sky, with a little tail behind it, flashing across the heavens? The white men call it a comet, but we know what it is. It is Fire Tiger. He is showing his power out of the water, up in the sky.

He watches us all. WATCH OUT FOR FIRE TIGER! How can you keep him happy? Make him an offering. Have

46

your father take some tobacco and put it in his pipe. Then have him blow the smoke up in the sky at night so Fire Tiger can smell it. Fire Tiger may leave you alone—for a while—if you do that. He may even decide he likes you and break up a storm for you while he's up there. Or help you catch a fish in the river. If you're lucky.

THE LOVERS OF HANGING ROCK

Is your scalp prickly yet? No? Then I will tell you another story. This one is not from long ago. It really happened, so they say, on the Wabash river, where the Salamonie runs into it. If you go there, you will see a big rock cliff high above the river. It is called hanging rock.

A fair Indian maiden had two young men in love with her, the one the band chief's son, the other a Shaw-nee who had been adopted by the tribe. She was a proud woman. She would not say which of the men she really loved. Instead, she said, "You may fight a duel over me." The idea of two men fighting over her pleased the vanity of this cruel young girl.

The two young men came to hanging rock with the maiden on a moonlit night. The braves had knives and tomahawks. They slashed at each other until the blood was spilled on Hanging Rock. They were wrestling at the edge of the cliff. Sweating and almost worn out, they moved toward the edge. Finally the band chief's son got on top and stabbed the Shaw-nee brave, who fell from the cliff.

"No, no," shrieked the Indian maiden. "You have killed the man I loved. I see now how cruel I was!" She, too, plunged off the cliff. Now they are together in the Pine Isle of the Dead. But some people say, by the light of the moon on the Wabash, that they can see shadows up there at hanging rock at certain times of the year. Very mysterious shadows, and hear strange noises.

You don't believe me? Well, let me tell you another tale about strange things. This is the Monster of Manitto Lake.

47

THE MONSTER OF MANITTO LAKE

Over to the west, by the larger Lake of the Boulders, Mock-sin-kic-kee, is a small lake. It has dark waters and when the moon shines on it, it looks very gray and scary.

This is a lake of bad luck. Indians stay away from it. Some say Fire Tiger himself has made it his home. Surely it looks like he has come to life, because many braves say they have seen a monster in the lake.

What does he look like? Some say like a huge water snake. Some say like a huge seal of the northlands, with a wide head and bugging eyes.

In my grandfather's time men going fishing said they saw the bad one, and that he was brown and spotted. They said he roared like a buffalo bull at them.

So I always stay away from Manitto Lake. Now, a Frenchman told me something not too long ago. He said some French traders had been fishing and pulled out a huge fish. It was a pike fish. He was taller than a man and weighed as much as a small bear, they said. They say now and then there are such huge fish in these northern waters.

This Frenchman thought the monster was this fish or his grandfather, seen from a distance. But if I were you I wouldn't believe that. I'd stay away from Lake of the Monsters.

My mother is telling me I had better stop telling these bad tales and end with one good one. So I will tell you the story of the corn god and the gift he gave to men.

HOW THE INDIAN PEOPLE GOT CORN

Once long ago red men were the only men in the forest. They could not find enough to eat. Oh, it is true they could eat the wild Jerusalem Artichoke. They could dig up the root of the water lily and put it in a cooking pit in the ground and roast it. They could gather wild rice if any was growing. And of course they could hunt and eat the meat of wild game.

But some years the people, the women and little ones of the camps, would nearly starve. The Indian peoples wondered how they would survive if animals got scarce.

So they called a grand council and tried to decide what to do. "We must find a new food," said the Great Chief. Send all the band chiefs out to scour the lands to find a food that will always be good for us, and not run far into the woods like the quail, bear and deer do.

The band chiefs went out to look. They were gone for months. Finally they returned to the big camp. "We could find no new food," they said.

"What will we do?" said the women and wee ones.

One of the men had not come back. Finally, just as the council fire was breaking up, he came in, panting from running so much.

"We thought you might never come back," the council said. "Do you—could you—find anything that will help us feed our people?"

"Let me tell you," the brave said. They gave him some food and he began his story. "I searched high and low. I went to the far south, down the Great River. I myself was almost starving and I had found nothing, no, not from anyone I asked or any field I searched in.

"Finally I sat alone by the ashes of a dying campfire. Then I thought, I have been asking the wrong people. I should have asked the Great Spirit. Great Spirit, can you send us good food so our families will not starve?

"Suddenly a tall man stood before me. He was the handsomest man I have ever seen. His limbs were fine and strong, his hair the color of sand.

" 'You must fight me. If you kill me, it is well. Bury me where we fought.'

"I do not wish to fight you, I said. You have done nothing to wrong me.

" 'Yet you must. So the Great Spirit has decreed.'

"So I fought him and I won. Sadly I buried his body and as soon as I had done that, I looked at the ground. A shoot was appearing. Then a stalk shot up. At the top of the stalk, there as I watched, was an ear forming. Grains began to fill it out. Over it all was a tassel of fine silky hair like the handsome man's.

"I tasted the grain in this ear and it was delicious. As I was eating, the other grains dried in the ear. But then new ears formed on the plant and I picked all of them. I have brought them back to you. This is corn, from the Corn Spirit."

So ever after, we all may eat the wonderful corn that the spirit has sent and give thanks to the Great Spirit for his gift.

My mother is waving her hand at me ever so gently. I guess that means that is all I have to say. Let someone else tell a tale now.

In the 1830's George Winter painted a picture of a trap people set to capture a lake monster.

Chapter Four

The Priest's Tale: Religion and War

Nobody speaks for a long time after A-son-da-ki sits down.

The moon has completely vanished again under a cloud bank. The only light in the clearing is the sputtering fire. The men who were dancing have gone to the cooking pots to get food. They now sit before the embers silently eating. A strange quiet has settled over the clearing.

Then, finally, the Meda priest himself stands up.

It is getting late. Only at this late hour and without a moon can a Meda priest speak. I shall tell you things, strange things, hidden things because tonight is the magic night of the Corn Spirit. But if you say I said them, I will say I did not. Only you may hear them, and only tonight.

The Meda priesthood is the oldest order in this land. We are older than these Protestants, these Quakers and Methodists who come among us. We are older than the white man's church of Rome—the Catholics. It started only seventeen hundred years ago.

But Meda priests are from the oldest times. The Del-a-wares say that thousands and thousands of years before now, our Indian peoples came from the land far away across the ocean. They say we walked through snow and ice over land that is not there now and came into the new woodland world.

We walked so far some were tired and stopped in the land of Canada. Others walked here. Some kept going and went all the way to what you call Mexico. If they did, the Meda priests were with them.

We are priests because our fathers were priests. We talk to the Manittos, we talk to the Great Spirit. We give you Indian peoples the things that you need to make the spirits work for you. These are secret things so I cannot tell you all of what they are.

But perhaps, just perhaps, you wish to be healed of a sickness. First, you would call the old women and they would put a hot patch of herbs on you, mustard or elm bark, and it would make you better. If it did not, you could call the shaman. He is the medicine man, who comes to drive out the evil spirits with his spells.

Medicine Bag and Sacred Objects

Eagle Foot

Wooden Spoon

Eagle Feather Fan

Whistle

Otter Skin Bag

Ginseng

Herb Bag

Bear Claws

Pipe Bowl

Black Stone

But if he cannot work, you can call finally on a Meda priest. We will make it possible for you to talk to the Great Spirit himself.

To talk to Him, an Indian must first purify himself. Perhaps he will take a ritual bath. He will put himself in a steam house, where rocks are made hot with fire and then dropped into water. He will sit, thinking of the Great Spirit as long as he can and letting the steam come around him and then, when he can stand it no longer, he will go and jump into the stream ouside.

Or, he will stay out by himself to pray for purification. He will not eat or drink. Food and drink in the belly keep us from knowing the Great Spirit.

After a man is pure and ready to speak to the Great Spirit, he must find a way to approach him. That is where Meda Priests come in. We can do things that make men strong in spirit. If a man wishes to be strong in spirit and move the gods, he comes to me or the other priests.

I will want to know about his medicine bag. I will ask him what special thing he saw in his Moon-in-the-wild. For whatever he saw, whatever his vision, is what his medicine bag is about.

If he saw in his vision or dream the great eagle, he will have an eagle feather in the medicine pouch. There will also be other things, things that mark special times in his life. Perhaps he fought his first battle with the tribe at Pebble River. There will be a pebble from the river in the bag.

Suppose he met the great leader Pontiac. Pontiac gave him a button of brass from his coat. It will be in the medicine bag. Perhaps he has a small clump of grass which has a meaning only he can know. Medicine bags are very secret. Not even a Meda priest can know all that is in a man's medicine bag.

All the things together have very special powers. Lying there in secret they bring much good medicine. It is as if they are praying to the spirits all the time in that little bag.

If a man is sick, I can chant about the medicine bag, I can ask the bad Manittos to go away and then I can introduce the man to the Great Spirit.

I am a doorman at the door of the high Spirit. With my chants, my prayers, the smoke that I send from out my pipe, I can announce the man, spread out the mat for him and bid him to come in. The man himself can tell the Great Spirit what he needs.

To understand the Manittos of this earth and the Great Spirit, you must understand mysteries. All Meda priests have lodges where you can become a member to understand the mysteries of the Manittos.

Do you see that big bark house at the top of the little hill? That is the Meda house. There are altars in the house. When you are about eleven, you are first made a member of the order. You will leave your father and mother for a long time and come to stay at the Meda Priest's lodge. There you will go to the first altar and worship. It is the altar of the brook. We call the order of the brook the first degree. Our sacred animals are otter and muskrat. Their pelts have great magic.

After you are older and have done brave things that prove you have the favor of the Manittos, you can go to the second altar. It is the altar of the stream. There are four altars, and the last one is the altar of the ocean. These are very, very secret things and I cannot tell you what happens inside the house when you join the medicine lodge of the Meda priest.

But when you are done, you can talk better to the Great Spirit. You know more about him. Thus we say you have more and better medicine. With white men medicine means something you take for a body sickness. With us it also means magic, or power.

Medicine is especially important when it is time for war. Then the priest has all the men who are going to the war to bring in their medicine bags to the council fire at night.

All put the bags in a pile and join hands above them. With the combined magic of all these bags, we can go to meet our enemies with courage. All the strength and magic of the bags goes into the tribe's spirits so that we can shoot bows and arrows straight, fire guns right.

War is always a sacred ceremony for us. Through it we show we are men. To get close to an enemy, to look him in the eye and not blink, perhaps to wound or hurt him is to steal his strength and make it your own.

White men wonder about our customs. In the old days, when we sometimes ate of human flesh, it was to gain the strength of the person we ate. The old ones believed it was really good to eat a heart, because that is the seat of bravery in the body. We do not do this any more. The priests have come among us and told us it is wrong.

But taking a scalp is not the same. The white man taught Indians to take scalps in his wars in America. So many scalps from the enemy, so many dollars. We did not think of it first.

The only way we can go to war is if the men of the council decide so. Perhaps the Shaw-nees will send us a war belt. It will be of black beads and will have writing or pictures on it. They will tell what the reasons for going to the war are. We will ask the Shaw-nee to sit among us before the camp-fire and smoke. Then each band chief will be asked his idea about the war.

You do not have to speak, but most men there do. When all have spoken, the man who is the war chief for the tribe will tell what will happen. War, or peace.

If war, we must get ready. The women must fill the knap-sacks. Put in cooked corn and maple sugar and dried beef. Then, the night before we go, we must dress ourselves for war. We pluck out all hair except on the top of the head. This we call the scalp lock. We dress the lock up with beads and feathers of eagles. We paint red, yellow, black, as our vision tells us to paint.

We put on the breech clout. This is a piece of deerskin or wool we hang from a sash at the waist and pull between the legs. We hang a gun and powder horn from a short string over the shoulder. We hang the knife we carry from a string around the necks. And so we are ready.

But before we put the weapons on, we must dance the war dance. The men who will be going dance slowly at first, then build up speed and strength. Harder, ever harder they dance. Their faces show the strain. They must feel the reason for the war in their hearts and the faces will show it. On, on they go until the dawn comes and the sun rises. Now they are angry enough to fight.

We carry more than knife and gun. We carry a war club, carved, with a ball on the end. And we will have war bows and arrows, with the arrow shaped so it can go into a man well.

But before we can fight, of course, there is the trip along the war path. We have worn these paths bare over many hundreds of years, from north to south from the Great Lakes to Ohio and south. From Appalachian mountains to the Mississippi, father of waters.

When we go, it is in single file, silently. Chief, men of wisdom and age and then the young men. And sometimes it happens that a young man from another tribe will wish to join the party. He feels in his heart that the cause is right. Or he wishes to show that he is a man.

The man from another tribe must walk behind us all. He must camp away from the others. Finally, one day, on the path, he will approach the chief and ask if he may join. The chief may take him or not.

Then there will be the carrying boy. This is a young man who has not yet won his war feathers. He will bear the food and camp supplies.

There is a thing that you may think odd. That is that a woman may come to war now and then. I have known it that a woman has come to me, the Meda priest, and said that she has had a dream. In the dream she saw that she led the warriors. They came to the enemy camp and they came by surprise. All the enemy came out of their bark huts. They could not aim or shoot. The strange thing is that later we let the woman lead and her dream came true. When Manitto sends a dream, we should obey it, even if it is a woman who has it.

And so, painted, we go to the camp of war. We do not fight in battles as you French do. How silly you look and act, marching across an open field. You stand in your lines, you kneel and aim your guns. You put yourself right in front of the enemy. And he mows you down like grass.

No, we fight with our heads. Stand behind trees and wait until the group of enemy men come past. Jump out and on them. Or run down on a village when dawn has come. That is how we win. It shows more sense than the white man's war.

When the battle is over, we take the things we want from the village. Earrings we can all wear, bracelets for the women and men, weapons. And we carry the dead and wounded away with us.

Sometimes we do not win, and then we must leave fast. The Manittos sent my own father good luck when he was wounded and the tribe lost. Here is what happened. My father was aged and chose to go with the war party. When a man is old, he may say whether he wants to go or not. It is up to him. And a Meda priest does not always go with the war party, even if he is young.

My father was a brave man. We went to war and he was wounded with several arrows. The men carried him off after the battle. But the enemy was coming. My father said, "Leave me here. You must go on fast, and I will die anyway. I order you as a priest of the tribe."

The men listened and did what my father said. They left him. "Sit me beyind this tree and face me toward the village," my father said. "That way I will die looking toward those I love."

The odd thing was, he did not die. The enemy men went right by and did not see the old man behind the tree. And finally, he said, a strange man came along and stopped his bleeding by putting metal in his wounds. He felt better. He got up the next day and walked home.

Everybody thought he was dead and had sung the death song for him. They thought he was a spirit when he came walking in. After that people believed he really was the greatest Meda priest of all. They asked him all the questions about life and death and put him at the highest place at the corn feasts.

Who was the warrior who came like a miracle man to help my father as he sat behind that tree? He did not ever know. But perhaps it was the Son of the West Wind himself.

They say he helps the good man. And who can be a better man than a Meda priest?

Although war is a big thing in our lives, it has always been done in a small way. By this I mean that we go in small groups to do battle with other tribes. Only a few at most will be killed. And then they come and do the same to us.

But when you French, English, Americans fight you have huge battles. You bring out hundreds, thousands of men with musket guns. Cannons boom. The air is filled with gun smoke. You cannot even see the clouds when white men fight because the air is filled with yellow smoke.

It is hard for us to fight that way. We cannot win. There are many more whites and one tribe, even the Miamis, cannot hope to beat them. But Little Turtle has the right idea now. He says we all must get together, all tribes, and fight as one.

That will be hard, because we fight each other so much. It is not easy to fight next to a Shaw-nee or Pot-a-wat-o-mi who has killed your brother in a raid just last year.

But we must do it. We must forget old battles with the Indian brothers and look to the new ones, with the white man. Only then can we drive him away.

I think about it much, this coming in of the white man. I talk about it much when I talk to the Great Spirit as priest.

The other day as I was in the sweat lodge I prayed. "Great Spirit, tell me what will happen to the Miamis and other Indians."

I waited a long time. Finally I thought I heard a voice in my mind, like the voice of the water from a brook bubbling up.

"All things change. On the tree is a bud, then a full green leaf, then a bare branch again. But as the old leaf falls, it makes the soil rich. And soon a new bud comes again."

What does that mean? Even I as a priest am not sure. I think it means there will be changes for the Miamis. I do not

59

want us to be like the fallen leaves. But if we are, new buds will come again. Perhaps that is what the bubbling voice was saying. "The Miamis cannot die, only change. If they fall, they will grow and bloom again, as long as they are strong in spirit." I pray it will be so.

Chapter Five

Little Turtle's Tale: Politics of the Miamis

The crowd of men, women and chidren at the Harvest Festival has slowly drifted away. The fire is burning into embers. The priest, after finishing his tale, sits for a long while by the edge of the woods. Then he and the Frenchman join a few men slowly smoking their pipes before the remains of the fire.

The French trader has not spoken much this evening. So many Miamis have told their tales to him. Now it is his time to talk.

"I am learning much about this Miami tribe. It is well I do so, because I know other tribes of the northlands. I am from Montreal. I do speak your language well enough to be understood, but this is my first time to Ke-ki-on-ga and the land of the Miamis."

"Brother," says the priest, "you know you are welcome. We will have many furs to trade you tomorrow. Trading with the French brings good fortune to us all, no? What more can we offer you in the name of the Manittos? Ask what you will and because it is the festival of the harvest I will try to grant it."

"Yes," says the French trader. I have a wish. Now, what I would ask of you is that you let me meet the man I have heard of from all."

"Who is that?" asks the priest.

"The most famous Miami of them all. The Little Turtle."

The priest does not change his look. "I do not know. The Little Turtle is in his own shelter tonight preparing a messenger for important business. Still, I have promised to give you a wish. I shall try."

After a time the priest returns with a man of short stature and a strong-looking face

The trapper rises. "Me-she-kin-no-qua," he says, in a voice that shows he is impressed. He has heard that this is the greatest Indian chief in America.

The chief and the trader sit down and the trader asks for a tale. Little Turtle thinks for a while and they says yes. "For, if I give a tale on the night of the Harvest, the Manittos will give good fortune to me and my family all through the winter. So our people believe," he says.

The trapper looks into the solid, serious face. The tale begins.

I was named Painted Terrapin, the bright land turtle of the path and garden plot. My mother said it was because I was mottled, spotted all the day of my birth, like the turtle is. You white man could not translate that, so they called me Little Turtle.

Shall I tell you how I got to be war chief? It was in the days of La Balme, one of your kind, Frenchman. This was a puffed up man who fought for the Americans in the Revolutionary War.

The British held Detroit and this La Balme led some Frenchmen and Indians to try to take it. He came to Eel River, near here. La Balme wanted to burn our home village and chase the Indians away.

When I heard of it, I was angry. I called together some young warriors. "Let us attack these fat French villagers 'this

Indians attack a Kentucky fort.

La Balme leads and stop them from burning Ke-ki-on-ga and going to Detroit. They do not belong in our woodlands."

The warriors looked grave. "These are the Americans' friends the French. They are on horseback. What are we against so many in a well-armed party?"

"They are village pigeons, I tell you. Like the pioneers. Growing fat by their firesides pecking corn. One Indian with a strong spirit is equal to any ten white men. Their spirits are puny," I said. "Besides we will surprise them."

We came to Eel River and found the Frenchmen and other men asleep. Puny pigeons! They had not ever posted a guard. And there were Indians among them! We killed them all, except one that we made captive.

Men have asked me how I succeed in besting the white man when others fail. I will tell you.

The spirit called Thunder Bird has given us rules of war. They are these: Know your enemy and try to out-think him. Then, if you cannot out-think him, fight him in a fair fight. Go swiftly, kill quickly and act fairly. This we did at Eel River and we won. And if you cannot beat your enemy in a fair fight? Then find a way to live in peace. Those are the rules of Thunder Bird.

We Miamis do not do well when we break the rules of war. My cousin was along on the raid on the Kentucky fort ten summers ago, and I tell you the tribes did not fight as the Bird of Thunder taught us. Perhaps they are hearing the white man talk too much. Let me tell you how it went, then you will see no great chief led them.

The English general led many Pot-a-wat-o-mis, Shaw-nees, Miamis and some others to Kentucky, to frighten the Americans there and destroy the forts. We Indians fight against the Americans because we do not want them in our land. We thought maybe the British could run them off. There were cannons and British soldiers too.

Their women and children hoed the cabbages outside the walls of the fort. The British general hid in the woods at night. We crept forward at dawn and surrounded the fort. Inside, they began firing. Our Indians stood behind a cannon and when it fired, it smashed the blockhouse at the side of the fence. An American man came out. He wanted to make a truce with the British general. They agreed to give up the fort. We said we would not hurt them.

All well and good. I hate Americans as much as any man and war is war. We should have killed their men in battle, and burned the fort so they could not use it. Then we should have moved quickly on to burn all the forts in Kentucky. That would have been a good lesson.

Maybe then they would have left. But then what did we all do? I do not like to tell you because it would make the Thunder Bird cover his face with his feathers.

We went inside. Our Indians started running. Their hatred of the Americans overcame their good sense. They began chasing women around, children too. They killed babies with tomahawks and threw them into the fire. One mother, so it is said, tried to pull her baby off the fire but an Indian killed her too and threw her on the fire.

I am sorry to say the Miamis went mad with looting. Instead of going on to another fort, they spent their time taking things. They took clothing, jewelry, money. They stuffed everything they could carry into their packs. everything else in a big pile and burned it, dogs, chairs, plates and cups. They killed anybody who got in their way, even the brave ones, whom the Thunder Bird says must be spared.

The British General said it was all too much. He tried to stop the Indians but he could not. My own cousins began to line up many women and children and take them as prisoners. It was not a good idea to take these weak ones. We marched them up to Detroit and we did not have food for them or us either. We did not attack more forts.

And the Kentuckians got together and brought an army down to punish us. It was all a waste. We did not fight as Thunder Bird told us. Strike quickly, kill men fairly, move on to fight again. You must fight with your brain or you will never win.

The Americans say we are cruel. Brutal savages they call us. But I have seen them just as cruel. To get even, George Rogers Clark burned our homes, ruined the corn for winter, burned the corn fields so our little ones would starve. And in Pennsylvania, Ohio, and Viriginia groups of white men came to Indian villages and killed women and children while they slept.

They do this because they hate us and we are on the land they want. "Red devils" they call us. Some Kentucky men say they will kill every Indian they see. They say they will not stop until each and every one of us is gone, wiped out.

Arthur St. Clair fought Miamis for George Washington and lost.

There is a man in Kentucky who brags in taverns that he has a suit made out of Indian skins. So they are cruel, too.

Of course it is fair to take prisoners. That is part of what the War Spirit gives you. But you must do it with good sense. You may take a few to serve the tribe as servants. They can do the women's work. Or hold them for ransom to get money or Indians back.

Sometimes we kill prisoners in camp. Sure it is that our brothers the Shaw-nees did that after George Rogers Clark burned their corn fields. The spirit of the corn had been hurt. They needed to make that up to him, to sacrifice one of the white men, they said.

We Miamis do not burn prisoners at the stake much anymore. What we do is to test their manhood. All Indians do that. The Shaw-nees and Del-a-wares all line up in camp, women and children too, and make a tunnel. A prisoner must run through this path of people. All the people try to hit him, make fun of him to see how brave he is. They have sticks and clubs and try to hit him while he runs.

At first it is easy to run, but as the blows fall on your legs, it is harder. When a weak one falls, badly wounded from the blows, the women finish the job and kill him right there with tomahawks.

But often a man survives the tunnel. He comes to the end and is still standing. If he makes it, one in the tribe may claim him for a servant. Or as husband, brother, son. If a man or woman has lost a son, he or she may say "I want this man for my own son."

We Miamis do not have the gauntlet tunnel, as you call it. No, one brave in the tribe fights hand-to-hand with the prisoner. If the prisoner wins, another brave will fight him, then another. If the prisoner fights bravely, finally he will be adopted into the tribe.

When that happens the new son is treated oh, so well. He is taught everything that the father knows, loved and cared for, given the best food.

You think we treat our captives badly? You are wrong. Once they live with us a while, many do not wish to go home. They love the life we lead. The fishing, hunting, freedom by the pretty streams and woods. We have festivals, we live together as friends.

Ask one who was a captive if you do not believe it. Oh, many will say they do not like being with us. But many others have refused to be traded back when the whites came to get them.

I should know. I have an American son. Let me tell you about him. William Wells was the name of the boy the warriors found on a raid in Kentucky a few short years back. They brought him back on horseback to Ke-ki-on-ga and he fought them all the way. He had no fear. Whenever they stopped, he ran for the woods until they tied his hands together behind his back.

William Wells was a hero to both whites and Indians. An Indian captive who became the loved son of Little Turtle, he returned to the whites and died leading a group being attacked by Indians away from Fort Dearborn.

When they returned to camp, I took him for my own son. He would not eat along the trail and I took him into the bark hut and sat beside him. I said nothing but gave him cooked Jerusalem artichokes, you call them. He shot me a sour look and pushed them away. I shrugged and left and when my back was turned, he reached for them and ate. Did he eat! He ate the whole pot.

When I came back he said nothing for a long while. Then he pointed to the pot as if to ask what root was in it that he had liked.

"A-pe-kon-it," I told him, using our name.

"A-pe-kon-it." He said the name over and over.

Finally he said his new Indian word so much that we called him "A-pe-kon-it."

And so he was adopted into the Miamis. The women took him to the stream and scrubbed his body with sand. This was to get the white blood out of him. When he glowed red, we could take him to the council fire. I told the council my wish to have him for my son.

And so he has been now for many years. I took him to the woods to hunt mos-wa. I showed him how to crush the mint leaves to mask his smell, to make the deer bleat call with the whistle that we have, how to walk without noise and through the water. He learned as fast as the wind in spring and soon we had deer meat in the pot.

Now he is a better hunter than the Indians here! He knows, how well he knows, to talk to the spirit, the Manitto of the deer. To tell it he is sorry that he has to kill it, but that he has hunted it in a fair fight.

And yet, I do not think my A-pe-kon-it is Miami at his heart. When he shoots a bow or throws a tomahawk, his arm is Indian. When he walks the trail with his ear sharp for every twig that snaps, and sends his voice into the trees to sound like an owl, his mind is Indian. But his heart is white. Sometimes I know he thinks of the white men in Kentucky and Indiana. Perhaps he misses the white man things, the wheat bread, the roast cow, the soft feather bed.

He knows the white men are making an army. The white man does not like what the Miamis and other tribes have been doing in Kentucky, Ohio and Indiana. It is said we have killed near to two thousand of them, driven off twenty thousands of their horses. For us it is a matter of life and death. We cannot live without the hunting grounds and we will do all we can to drive the white man out of them.

And so they are angry. Near the Ohio River they camp and build a fort. They wish to march to battle, to drive the Indians out. The Great White Father, George Washington, has said that it is time to beat us.

The day is coming soon. We will fight as we have never fought before.

All about Ke-ki-on-ga, trader, you have seen the Indians. Del-a-wares, Mun-sees, even some Shaw-nees camp about our Miami wigwams. The whites have pushed them out, and they wish to come to where the war chiefs are.

We will get the war totem, send the belt of war about to other tribes, to the Pot-a-wat-o-mis, even, perhaps the Kick-a-poos. They will come and there will be battle with these whites. And my son, my A-pe-kon-it, my William, will have to choose.

What if he should choose the whites? Ah, I would understand. A man must stand by his clan, his family. All our families have clan names from animals. Be it turtle, wolf, or bear it is the sign of our family clan. And white Kentuckian is A-pe-kon-it's clan. Perhaps he will go to fight with the Kentuckians. That would be loyalty. I will be proud. What else could I expect of Little Turtle's son?

It will not be easy to win from George Washington's soldiers. Sometimes I think about the white man and I wonder. He has boxes that tell the time with little hands, brushes made of pig hair to clean his teeth, saddles of the finest leather. But most of all he has guns, many of them.

We are getting good at shooting guns, and we have a few. But George Washington has hundreds. No, thousands of guns. All kinds. He has the large round ones of brass that shoot the shot. They call them cannons. He has the Kentucky long rifles, oiled and slick as bear grease. He has pistols and muskets.

We will follow Thunder Bird's rules. We will think first. Then we will think again. We will be clever. Catch his army when they are not looking. When they are tired and want to go home. We will attack the supply trains so we can stop the march and starve them out.

And when it comes to battle, we will think too. We will find the best place of all, hide, surprise, be very careful. We will go quickly, strike hard with the best men, shoot well, leave at once to strike again.

And we will win, because Thunder Bird's rules are good, and because the Indians have the power of good magic in all we do.

The white men are many. They are like the mice that come into a field after a mild winter. Thousands, and then thousands more. A wolf, even a hungry wolf and his mate cannot eat all the mice. There are too many. Still, we will try. And after we have done all Thunder Bird's rules, after we have thought, and fought and done all like men, then what if we do not win? If we do not win, perhaps we will try the last.

"Try to make peace and do it well." That is what he says. That is what we will do.

The Battle of Fallen Timbers in 1791 in Ohio saw the Indians lose a major battle. In the treaty which followed, they were forced to give up much land.

Chapter Six

War Comes to The Miamis

We must leave the harvest campfire of the Miamis and follow their history from that time until now.

Little Turtle was right. War was coming to the Miamis. President George Washington knew that he must break the power of this tribe in what are now the states of Ohio and Indiana. Otherwise, settlers could never come in.

He organized an army, as Little Turtle said he would. In 1790, in October, General Josiah Harmer led an army made mostly of pioneer men up to Ke-ki-on-ga, the Indian homeland. It was not a good army. There were many old men and young boys. They didn't like staying in lines and they talked back to Harmer when he gave an order.

When Harmer's army got to Ke-ki-on-ga, only a few Indians were there. They were away on a fall hunt. Harmer finally sent Colonel Hardin to look for Indians. Little Turtle got the Miami men together and hid them in an ambush northwest of Ke-ki-on-ga. When Hardin and his men came by, the Indians fired on them suddenly. The Indians made a ring around the pioneers and shot all but one. Little Turtle had been right. He had out-thought the enemy and he had won.

Meanwhile back at Ke-ki-on-ga, General Harmer was burning the town. Cornfields, fences, beans, pumpkins, bark homes—he destroyed them all.

72

Harmer was determined to beat the Indians. He ordered most of the army to march away a few miles south. Then he told Hardin, who had already lost one battle that day, to sneak back and try to trap the Indians when they returned to their homes at Ke-ki-on-ga.

But Little Turtle was still thinking. He did not want to be trapped. He sent a small group of Indians to lead Hardin's frontier soldiers away and then jumped on the white men that were left. The Indians fought well until finally Hardin's men came back. They were mad that they had been fooled and fought hard.

By the time the battle was over the white men had lost 183 killed and many wounded.

That night there was victory dancing around Miami campfires.

But George Washington was not about to give up. In 1791 he had a new general named General St. Clair build a chain of forts north through Ohio. Finally St. Clair came with about 2,000 men to where the Wabash River starts to flow in northern Ohio. It is not too far from the border of Indiana today. They began to build a big fort to beat the Indians once and for all.

But the Indians knew exactly what was going on. They had their scouts. Also, the British, who were still around, told them about the American plans.

Little Turtle got other Indian tribes together. He called a meeting of great chiefs: Blue Jacket of the Shaw-nees and Breaker-to-Pieces of the Del-a-wares. "We must drive out this St. Clair," he said.

Who would be chief? Breaker-to-Pieces said it must be Little Turtle, who was younger than he was and faster in battle.

Little Turtle thought again. What would be the best time to attack? When St. Clair's American troops were about to have their breakfast! They would be thinking about bacon and cornbread, not attack.

And so Little Turtle had all the Del-a-wares, Shaw-nees and Miamis hide in the woods near the American camp. The Indians were in trees, behind rocks. They began to fire at the men, who were out in the open. The Americans would fire back but they could not see the Indians.

So many Americans were killed there at Ft. Recovery that the ones who were left got scared. They were huddled in a circle in the middle of the camp and the Indians were closing in. Their officers were dead. So St. Clair's army decided to make a run for it.

They began to retreat and they began to run faster and faster. They dropped everything they had, packs, food, even guns.

The Indians under Little Turtle chased them for four or five miles. When the Indians stopped they realized they had a major victory. They had beat an American army twice their size. They had killed 593 men and 31 officers. They had wounded many, too.

This was the biggest victory ever gained by Indians over American troops. It was more important than Custer's Last Stand. George Washington's army had been defeated by the brave and clever Little Turtle. For the time being, the Indians would be left alone.

Some people in Congress thought America should just forget about having Indiana, Ohio, Illinois and Michigan in the U.S.

"It's too dangerous. Let the Indians have it," they said.

But Washington didn't listen. He looked around for the best, bravest and smartest general he could find to go back and beat Little Turtle and the other Indian chiefs.

"Go get me Mad Anthony Wayne," Washington said to one of his helpers. Mad Anthony Wayne was a general from the Revolutionary War. He was so fearless some people thought he was half-crazy. He would do things nobody else would think of doing to get victory. That's why they called him Mad Anthony.

In 1793 Mad Anthony Wayne began organizing a super army. "I'm not going out there against those Indians until every last man in my army understands what it is to be tough and brave," Wayne said. "Drill till you think you're going to fall. Take sentry duty when it's cold and don't complain. Learn to eat little and march far."

Little Turtle was busy too. He was going around trying to get other tribes to help the Miamis. The Miamis were in charge. Finally the Indians appeared outside the strong fort Wayne had built. They hoped to find some cannons they had hid in the bushes when they beat St. Clair. But the Americans were now thinking too. They had found the cannon and took it inside.

The Indians attacked some soldiers who were outside but they couldn't get into Wayne's strong fort.

Now the Indians began to argue. "We should fight soon and in the open with these white men. Bring them out here and we'll mow them down," they said.

But Little Turtle thought they should not do this. "You can't beat a general like Wayne who always sleeps with one eye open," he said. Let's go back to the woods and cut off his supply trains. Starve him out. Do it little by little."

Nobody wanted to listen to Little Turtle. The Indians decided to risk all on a big open battle. Little Turtle shook his head, but he knew he could not make them listen to him.

Mad Anthony Wayne's army went forward, building more forts as they went. They were coming nearer and nearer to Ke-ki-on-ga and the very land where the Miamis had their homes.

Finally the white army came to a place known as Fallen Timbers. Big logs were all over the ground because a tornado had blown through. Here the Indians were in ambush. They were ready to do battle to stop the whites from going any further.

But Wayne was ready. He gave orders for his cavalry, his men on horseback, to ride out. They went in back of the

Indians on both sides and surrounded them. They chased the Indians for over two miles.

Finally the Indians saw they could not win and went in all directions. Little Turtle had been right. They could not win a big open battle.

Wayne started marching west, heading for the villages near Ke-ki-on-ga. He burned corn fields as he went, so the Indians would have no food supplies for a new attack.

He was surprised at how many fields the Miamis had. "I never saw such immense fields of corn in any part of America," he said. And there were so many Indian villages.

He got to Ke-ki-on-ga. He ordered a fort to be built there and when it was finished it was named Fort Wayne after him.

The Indians felt beaten and went into the woods. "This Wayne is A-lang-sang, The Wind," they said, because he was so fast and strong. But the Del-a-wares called him "The Blacksnake" and hated him.

A new treaty was signed at Ft. Greenville in Ohio in 1795. In it the Miamis gave up a good deal of land in Ohio and Indiana and promised to be peaceful.

Little Turtle was as wise in peace as he was in war. "Make a good peace," Thunder Bird had told the Indian peoples, and Little Turtle tried to obey him.

"We must now change our ways," Little Turtle said. "The white man has won in a fair fight. We must live in peace with him whatever that means."

Little Turtle did not like the white man's ways. The traders and soldiers gave the Indians much whiskey and rum and they drank it too much. When they drank, like many people, they fought and got into trouble. Little Turtle asked the states of Kentucky and Ohio to stop people from selling whiskey to Indians.

He went to talk to the Congress of the U.S. "Liquor is more to be feared than tomahawks," he told the Congress of the U.S. While he was there, he saw people getting smallpox

76

shots. He got a shot himself and asked for doctors to come to his people so they would not get smallpox any more. He saved many lives this way.

After the Battle of Fallen Timbers, Little Turtle came to think the Indians should learn to farm and raise hogs and chickens. "We can no longer hunt in these lands," he told the Miamis. We must learn to live as the white man lives now." The Indians did not like to raise hogs very much. Most of them never did become very good farmers.

There wasn't much to do in the Indian camps after Fallen Timbers. Many of the young men were unhappy. There weren't any more great hunts and Moons-in-the-wild. Some Indians began wearing pants and jackets like the white men. Some of the young men began playing dice and cards.

Things were starting to change. Many white pioneers were coming into Southern Indiana and Illinois. The Governor of these areas was William Henry Harrison. He lived in Vincennes. He began getting the Indians to sign treaties. Millions of acres of land were signed away. The Miamis signed, too.

Two Indian brothers began to ride around talking to the Indians about how bad things were starting to get for the Indians. The white man was getting all the land. The Prophet was the name of one brother. Te-cum-seh was the name of the other. They were both Shaw-nees.

In camps of the Shaw-nees, Del-a-wares, and Miamis, warriors gathered around these two brothers. First, the Prophet would speak. "Brothers," he would say to the Indians, "I am sent by the Great Spirit to tell you how to act. You are too much like the white man. You drink his whiskey. You wear his silver jewelry. You hunt for him. The Great Spirit wants you to stop all this. Go back to being Indians."

The Prophet, whose name was Tens-kwat-a-wa, said he had some dances sent by the Great Spirit for them to do. He

77

had some beads and chants that would make them good Indians again.

But his brother had another thing to say. Te-cum-seh was a tall, strong-looking Indian who could give a good speech. He was a real leader, one of the great ones of American history.

"My brothers," he would say to the Indians. "The Americans have taken all our land. They give us a few cooking pots and some wormy wheat and whiskey in return. We should get together and really drive them out."

Little Turtle told the Miamis not to listen to Te-cum-seh and The Prophet. "We have tried all that," he said to the young men. "There are too many white men and they have excellent weapons and leaders. We must settle down and do the best we can as farmers."

But Te-cum-seh rode far and wide. He rode to Wisconsin, to Michigan, even to Canada. Everywhere he told the Indians they must all get together. "We have had enough. Drive the whites out," he said.

Governor Harrison did not care for that at all. He told Te-cum-seh to come and see him in August of 1810. Te-cum-seh came with seventy-five braves and sat under a tree in front of the Governor's house.

"A few bad Indians have made these treaties," Tecumseh said. "You are taking everything. You want to drive us into the Great Lakes so we will have nowhere to go."

The Governor tried to answer Te-cum-seh, but that just made the Indian angrier. Te-cum-seh jumped up. The governor jumped up. The Indians reached for their tomahawks. The troops from Vincennes reached for their pistols. Then everybody calmed down.

But it was sure that war was on the way again. Te-cum-seh went south to get the Creeks and other southern Indians to join him. He thought that when he came back, there would be a huge battle with all the whites in Indiana and Ohio. If he had all the tribes, he could win.

He left his brother The Prophet at a new village he set up where the Tipp-e-canoe River enters the Wabash. It is near where Lafayette is now. Lots of Indians and their families came there. Some Miamis came, too. Many stayed with Little Turtle, who didn't like Te-cum-seh.

William Henry Harrison took an army from Vincennes up to The Prophet's village. He wanted to show that the Americans were strong. They weren't going to be afraid of Te-cum-seh.

In the Indian camp, the Miamis and other Indians did not think Harrison would really fight. Te-cum-seh had told his brother The Prophet not to fight, but some of the Indians in the camp wanted battle.

Win-nam-ac, a Pot-a-wa-to-mi, demanded that the Indians mount an attack. "They are only a day away, marching along the river," he said. "We must go out to them." Stone Eater, a Miami trained by Little Turtle himself in warfare, wondered if it was a good idea.

A black worker from Harrison's army came into camp. He was not afraid of Indians. In fact, he told them that the Americans had no cannons.

"They are just fooling us. They do not wish to fight," The Prophet told all the Indians in camp.

But the next morning, November 6, the white man's army led by William Henry Harrison was at Tipp-e-canoe.

The Prophet sent some Indian scouts to Harrison's camp, which was nearby. When they returned, they said, "The White Chief Harrison says he wants only peace. Yet war is in his eye. He says we should send some of our chiefs to him tomorrow to talk about peace."

"Yes!" said Win-nam-ac. "We can fool this white man. The Great Spirit has sent him into our hands. We will take pistols beneath our coats and shoot him at the meeting."

Two Win-na-ba-go Indians said they would go and kill Harrison. But Stone Eater of the Miamis said, "It is not a good idea. If we must attack, let it be tonight, when the fires are bright. We can see their faces if we go up quietly through the woods. We will be able to catch them by surprise. Now, quickly, when they are not ready. Little Turtle would have done it that way."

There were two British officers in the camp. They were trying to stir up trouble. The War of 1812, when Britain fought the U.S., was about to happen. "No, we say wait until tomorrow. You can sneak up at dawn."

"No, no! We must listen to what Te-cum-seh, our War Chief has told us. He did not want us to fight at all. Unless we can be sure to win, we must not fight." So thought Stone Eater the Miami.

The talk about if and when to fight the army that waited nearby went on and on. The campfire blazed in the cold night; the clouds looked black overhead.

Finally Win-nam-ac said, "If you do not fight and fight soon, I am taking my troops away. I will not come back, no matter what you and your brother say."

The Prophet looked hard at Win-nam-ac. Then he stood up. "I am going away into the woods for a short while. I will talk to the Great Spirit. He will tell me what we should do. Now I will get ready for my trance."

He began to dance about. He took a bowl and went to the fire. He scooped up some hot coals out of the fire and began to roll them around in the bowl. He had some beads he said were magic around his neck and he began to touch them and sing. He was chanting "ay, ah, yah, yah" in a loud, wailing voice. Then he went off into the woods.

Finally The Prophet came back. "I have had my trance," he said. "The Great Spirit tells me we can attack. He says we can win. The bullets of the white man will have no effect on the Indians in this camp. They can fire, but the bullets will not hurt us. So says the Great Spirit."

All the Indians got ready to fight at dawn. They cleaned their guns. They tested their bows and arrows. They drank things which would empty their stomachs. It was good to go into battle on an empty, not full stomach.

Then they put their medicine bags in the center of the clearing and touched the pile to get the magic. There was not time to do more; dawn was only an hour or so away.

The Pot-a-wa-to-mi scouts came panting in. They hurried to tell Tens-kwat-awa what they had seen as they crept about the American camp. "General Harrison has ordered everyone to sleep on their guns. Their soldiers are green and young. They will run when we come."

Stone Eater the Miami was as ready as the rest. He put the paint of war on his face and gathered the small group of Miamis together. "As we have fought for Ke-ki-on-ga, we now fight for our Indian peoples. These white men wish to wipe us from the face of the earth. They think no more of us than of their dogs or pigs. Our children and wives are in danger. Let us fight for these wives and little ones. And for all the Indian people. We do not have a chance if these white men win."

All the Indians crept through the swamp near Tipp-e-ca-noe Battle Field. They could hear the army of Harrison getting up. They were making morning camp sounds. They were seeing to the horses, putting logs on the fire, getting cooking pots ready for corn meal mush.

The Indians were on their stomachs. One warrior shot, then another. The Americans in the camp were confused. Where were the shots coming from? The Indians wanted to circle the camp and cut off the Americans.

"I see General Harrison," one Indian whispered. Sure enough, there was a man on a gray horse like the one everyone said Harrison rode. The Indian took careful aim and grunted. The man on horseback fell over dead.

It was, of course, not Harrison. Another officer, Colonel Owen, had been riding a gray horse and the Indians had shot him by mistake.

The white men began to get together. They formed in lines. As dawn came, they began to see the Indians. "We cannot allow them to surround us," all the soldiers shouted.

One officer, Colonel Jo Daviess of Kentucky wanted to go where the firing was hottest to drive the Indians away. But the Indians shot him and he soon died.

Both sides fought very hard. It was hard to tell which way the battle was going to go. The Prophet stood up on a huge rock near to the battlefield. He cried out and sang in a loud voice. He was praying to the Manittos, the spirits, to help the Indians. "I tell you that these bullets are not going to hurt you," he shouted to the Indians in the battle.

But many Indians were already finding out that what The Prophet said was not true. They were finding out the hard way. They were shot, wounded and killed, hundreds of them, there on the battlefield at Tipp-e-canoe.

But they were not the only ones. Many officers and men in William Henry Harrison's army were also wounded and killed by Indian bullets and arrows.

Finally the Indians began to fall back. The white man's army was stronger and could last longer.

Sadly Miamis, Pot-a-wat-o-mis, Kick-a-poos and all the rest saw they could not win. They began to move slowly through the swamp back to camp. One group of soldiers, called the Parke Dragoons from Vincennes got onto their horses. They made a final charge and the rest of the Indians fled. The Battle of Tipp-e-canoe was over.

Miami Indians like Stone Eater were right. When the white men won the Battle of Tipp-e-canoe, it was the beginning of the end for the Indians. The beaten Indians had to sign many treaties to give most all of their land to the goverment.

First one, then another signed. They had to. There was no choice.

The government tried to give them something in return. They got yearly payments called annuities as tribes. Each year government agents brought the money to them. They also had certain parts of the states reserved to them. These sections were called reservations.

"We must try for a good peace," the Miamis said. They gathered up their women and children and moved as far away as they could get from the pioneers. Fort Wayne was a growing village now. Beautiful Ke-ki-on-ga was a thing of the past. They would have to go far out, into the woods to get away.

Still, when the Miamis met other Indians they heard rumors. The Americans and British were going to war. Soon 1812 came and with it battles of the War of 1812. Te-cum-seh joined the British and tried to get the other Indians to keep on fighting. But Te-cum-seh was killed at a fight called the Battle of the Thames in Canada. So ended one of the brightest and best heroes in American history.

Little Turtle got sick and died. The Miamis were sad. A great chief had died, a war chief they would never forget. But Little Turtle was also a peace chief. He had taught them what Thunder Bird had taught him. When you can't win, you must make a good peace. The Miamis were trying.

But just about the time that Little Turtle died, the Miamis heard rumors. The war was coming to them in Indiana. There was one more last, big battle to be fought.

They looked again for the war paint and war totem.

"*Tell him he lies*," war chief Te-cum-seh says to William Henry Harrison in 1810. The scene was Grouseland, Harrison's home in Vincennes.

84

Chapter Seven

Later Days

The British and the Americans were fighting in 1812 in Canada and along the Great Lakes. The British really wanted the good fur trading lands. They thought they might be able to take back some of the land they lost in the Revolution.

Many Indian tribes joined the British. They thought they might get in on a good land deal if the British won the war. And anyway, they would do whatever they could to get even with the Americans they hated.

Some of the Indians who were for the British attacked pioneers in Ohio and Indiana and Illinois. Some Miami young men were part of the Indians that attacked, and some fought in battles. But many Miamis didn't want to be in the war.

William Henry Harrison was in charge of the western part of the American army. He was angry that the Indians were attacking pioneer cabins, burning them, stealing horses, sometimes killing the people inside.

He sent an officer named Campbell to clean out the Indians in Indiana to stop the raids. James Clarence Godfroy, a Miami who lived in recent times, told the story. It was passed down to him by his grandfather, who was there.

What he described is a battle called the Battle of the Mis-sis-sin-e-wa. It happened not too far from what is today Marion, Indiana, in 1812.

When James Clarence Godfroy told the story it went like this: "Campbell was working for Governor William Henry Harrison. He went looking for Indians who were causing trouble on the frontier. History says his orders were not to kill Indians unless he found them guilty.

"But Campbell wanted to be famous. The first group he came upon were a small band near Muncie. They were old men, women and children and a few cripples. He asked no questions but began to shoot them up. He killed a number of them.

"The Indians fled and started for Francis Godfroy's village. Campbell's army was close on their trail. The Indians went into camp and one of their fastest runners told their tale of woe. Chief Godfroy knew that these were good Indians and had kept their treaties.

"Godfroy thought that Campbell would march on the Miami villages and destroy them. He gathered warriors and went to locate Campbell.

"They surrounded the army of Campbell. Some of the Indians began to make sounds like owls and birds. The army knew they were surrounded. They began to shoot their guns at the tree tops. They couldn't see the Indians but they heard their sounds.

"After the pale faces had emptied their guns the Indians began to yell and holler. They emptied their guns on the whites.

"The army began to retreat and ran up the cliffs by the Mis-sis-sin-e-wa River. Many white soldiers ran right off the cliffs. Many broke through the ice on the river and were drowned.

" After daybreak the soldiers came back and buried their dead. Until a few years ago you could see the sunken places where the graves were."

The Indians felt they had fought hard and won a battle. It was their last. The War of 1812 was soon over. A new age began when the Americans won it.

Jean Baptiste Richardville, half-Indian, half-French, tried to help Indians make a transition to farming life.

The government came to the Indians and wanted the lands in northern Indiana and the rest of the states. Tens of thousands of pioneers began moving into the midwestern states in earnest now. They were no longer afraid of the Indians and they wanted to be in the "land of milk and honey, God's country," as they called the states we now live in.

Finally in the Treaty of St. Mary's the Miamis gave up a good part of their land in central Indiana. Parts of Ohio and a small part of Illinois and Michigan were also given up. In return they were given $15,000 a year, 160 bushels of salt, a blacksmith and a gunsmith to help them learn the white man's ways as fast as they could.

We can only try to imagine what life must have been like for these proud people of the woodlands after 1812. By 1818 147,000 people had moved into Indiana.

When the Miamis and other Indians went out to fish in the creeks, they met pioneer women washing their clothes.

When the men went to hunt wild turkeys or deer, they found frontier men had already scared them away. Cabins, barns, villages were going up on hills where they worshipped the Manittos.

However, some good-sized sections of land in northern Indiana, especially along the Wabash and Mis-sis-sin-e-wa, were still Miami property by the treaties. The name of the biggest reservations, where Miamis could go and live, were the Big Miami Reserve and the Thorntown Reserve. The Miamis went to live in these reservations to get away from the whites as best they could.

Some Miami men who had helped the whites or who had white blood received land grants. These men became the new chiefs of the tribe.

Several years before this a trader named Richardville had come from France to trade among the Miamis. He said he had come from a noble family in France. He married Te-cum-wah, a strong Miami woman who may have been the sister of Little Turtle.

Their son, Jean Baptiste Richardville, half-Miami, half-French, became one of the new chiefs of the Miamis. Jean Baptiste Richardville was a smart man who understood both the ways of the Indian and the ways of the white man. He often wore white man's clothing in his early days and could read and write well.

After the Treaty of St. Mary's, when so much land was given up, he began to wear Indian clothing again. He gave the rest of his life to seeing that the Indians were taken care of. Like Little Turtle, he knew that they must change their ways.

Jean Baptiste Richardville told the Miamis to work with the government. He helped set up schools and sent his own children to a school for Indians in Kentucky. The name of it was the Choctaw Academy.

Richardville built a house near Huntington, at what is called The Forks of the Little Wabash and Wabash rivers. Richardville really had more than one house. He travelled around trading and watching out for the Miamis.

He had an interesting family. One of his daughters was named La Blonde Richardville. She had blonde hair. Her son went to the Choctaw Academy and Richardville wrote letters to make sure his grandson was getting a good education.

People could not say Richardville's name very well. They said it "Russerville." The town of Russiaville is really named after the Indian chief, at least the way people said his name then.

Francis Godfroy was another chief in this later period. He was a mixed blood Indian, too. He had fought in the War of 1812 and was a war chief. After the war he was a merchant, had his own houses near Peru and in other places, and helped the Indians get their payments and watched out for them.

The payments became the most important thing in the Miamis' life after the War of 1812. After all, they could not make a living any more hunting and trading. How could they live?

The government wished them to farm, but they never took to farming very well. In Indian tradition women had always done the farming. They scratched the ground, put in the grain, hoed and harvested.

Miami men could not bring themselves to change the tradition. They did not like using horses and plows. And so, when the money arrived from the government it was a big day. With this money, the Miamis could feed their families. It could help to make up for the loss of their land and former free woodland life.

The $15,000 a year was divided up among members of the tribe. Chiefs like Godfroy and Richardville helped divide the money.

Francis Godfroy was also a French Miami. He lived near the Mis-sis-sin-e-wa River.

Sadly, though, the idea of giving the Indians annuity money did not work very well. What really happened was that a lot of traders and store keepers got the Indians to charge things. All year they sold them food and cloth and hardware on credit.

The prices were sometimes higher than they should have been, but not always. But people buy more than they should when there are "credit cards." The Miamis bought silver vases and fancy satin cloth and said "put it on my account." The Miamis just signed their X because most of them could not write.

Then, when the government money arrived, the greedy traders stood by the money table and made the Indians pay their charge accounts before they even got the money in their pockets. Many of the Indians could not believe they had charged so much. A lot of their money went out to the traders that first day.

Many of them were mad when they left the money table. They remembered how life used to be, before the stores took the money. They recalled the old life, the Moons-in-the-wild when they lived with nature and felt proud and free. Some remembered the proud times of Little Turtle, when the Miamis were feared by even George Washington himself.

They had won great battles over the United States western army. And now they stood at a table and paid over even the little they had to the white man's greed.

So the Miami men and women were sad at the payment time, They stayed around the villages and bought whiskey. Many traders had lots of whiskey for them to buy. Some Indians got very drunk, perhaps to forget the old days.

When they got drunk, they fought. Men and even women had knives and guns. Some were killed. Then everyone went home and felt miserable about it all. These were not good days for the Miamis.

Still, there were good times on the reservations. The forests were still beautiful, the lakes and rivers had fine fish in them and they could raise their families together as a tribe. Family life had always been important to the Miamis and now it became even more important. The reservation could be a good place.

The white man thought so too. Farmers who lived around the reservations of the Miamis began to look with jealousy at their Indian neighbors. These Indians, they said, were living on some of the finest farmland in the U.S.

Men who made a living buying land and selling it for higher prices than they paid for it looked at the Miamis' land too. "These Indians don't know how to use land," they said. "All they do is trap squirrels and fish and sit around and tell their old tales to their children. We should have that land. We could sell it for good prices."

Another treaty in 1826, which pushed the Indians into smaller areas yet, didn't help the Miamis. They were given more money, $25,000 a year. But they kept hearing that they had too much good land.

There was a new reason that the white men were grumbling and greedy for the Indians' land.

The settlers who were now farming in Indiana needed ways to get their crops to market, to sell them. They could use the rivers, but not everybody lived on a river. Many new roads were needed. And the Indians were on the land for the roads.

The Pot-a-wat-o-mis had to give the government the land they had to built the Lake Michigan Road from Logansport to South Bend. The Miamis had to give up some of their land for roads, too.

But that wasn't all. Out on the East coast, in New York State, they had built a wonderful canal to go where there were no rivers. It took passengers all the way to the Great Lakes and took all the crops to market. The Midwest wanted canals as fast as possible to carry their grain to market.

The Miami and Pot-a-wat-o-mi Indians lived on the very land which would be needed to built a canal. The canal the white men planned was going to go from the Maumee River at Fort Wayne to the Wabash. It was called the Wabash and Erie canal.

It really connected the Great Lakes with the Ohio and Mississippi, so it was a good idea. The problem was that its route was through many of the Miami villages that were left.

Irish workers came in to build the canal and mixed with the Miamis. Sometimes these workers and Indians got into fights with each other.

Soon several white groups began to say, "The Indian must go." They thought of a plan to send all the Indians to the West, beyond the Mississippi River. The Government in Washington passed a bill called the Federal Removal Act of 1830.

The President and Congress had some good things in mind when they passed this bill. They thought the Indians were going to be swallowed up completely by the whites. There would be no more Miamis. No more Del-a-wares, no more Pot-a-wat-o-mis.

Everybody would mix with everybody else. It was already happening to the Miamis. If all Indians went west, they could live together in their native way until they were ready to pick up new ways. But the plan caused pain and trouble to the Indians, who did not want to move. After all, they had been there before any white man.

The Del-a-wares had signed a treaty to get out of Indiana in 1821. They were long since gone. The Miamis' neighbors the Pot-a-wat-o-mis were forced to get out of Indiana in 1837, and had been marched to Iowa and Kansas through rain and blazing sun. Several, sick of cholera, an awful sickness, had died along the way.

Now Richardville and Godfroy and the other chiefs faced the fact that they were probably going to have to get out of Indiana too. They thought about how they could get the best deal on getting out. They went to council meetings with the government men to gain time. They promised nothing.

93

Finally, after the chiefs were sure the terms would be good for them, they signed a treaty on October 23, 1834, and another in 1838 near Fort Wayne.

The Miamis agreed to leave Indiana. Six chiefs would go and look at lands in Kansas. A final treaty signed in 1840 said they would leave within five years. The tribe got half a million dollars and the government said they would pay the terrible charge account money the Miamis owed the traders.

Some Miamis did not have to leave. The treaty said they and their children, about three hundred of them, could have good land in Indiana. These were people who had helped the government in earlier times. Richardville, now an old man, and his children and Godfroy's children got land and permission to stay.

The only large reservation still left belonged to the Miamis on the Mis-sis-sin-ewa. Their chief had been Met-o-cina. His son Mesh-in-go-me-sia now received the land for several villages.

It was not land the white man wanted anyway.

And so most of the Miamis got ready to leave the woodlands. "Our fathers lit their council fires from Detroit to the Ohio," the Miamis used to tell their children. Now the Miamis would have to light the council fires out west.

Jean Baptise Richardville finally died in 1841. The Miamis elected a new chief, Francis Lafontaine. He was at least half Miami, the rest white. It was his job to move most of the Miamis west. There were many problems and they did not start to go until 1846.

They were going to go most of the trip by water. They left from Peru, Indiana on October 6, 1846. There was much confusion as they got ready to leave their homelands. Relatives who weren't going came to say goodbye. Some white people came to "gawk" or sight-see and stare at the Indians.

They got on canal boats and went by canal to Ohio. When they got to the Ohio River, they got on a steamboat named the Colorado.

The Miamis went by steamboat to St. Louis, then up the Missouri River. They landed where Kansas City is today and got into wagons. Finally they came to their new home at Osage, Kansas, eight days later.

There were 323 Miamis who made it to Kansas. Chief Lafontaine went with the Miamis. After a while he had to return to Indiana on business, and there he died. But the Miamis went on anyway. Some of the Indians said they were surprised at how beautiful Kansas was. They said it looked in many ways like the Indiana homeland.

A few years later the Miamis and many other Indians who had been sent out of the Midwest were taken to Indian Territory, the name for a part of Oklahoma.

Back in Indiana, when it had been time to go, a few Indians couldn't stand to leave and ran away and had to be rounded up. A band named the Wau-wa-see band ran away to Michigan, but they were found and had to go west too. So eventually only the Miamis who had permission to stay were left in Indiana. There were over three hundred of them.

One Indian woman who got to stay back in Indiana has an interesting story. Her name was Mac-con-a-quah, which means Little Bear Woman. She was found in 1835 by a trader when she was an old woman living near the Mis-sis-sin-e-wa.

She was really white. Her name was Francis Slocum. She told part of her story to him and later it all came out. When she was five years old, she lived in the Wyoming Valley in Pennsylvania. The family homestead was attacked by Delaware Indians in 1778.

Francis, barefooted and crying, was carried off by a Del-a-ware. Her mother sobbed and cried as Francis was carried off. She was sure that Francis would die of cold and starvation on the trail in the hands of the Indians.

But Francis did not die. The Del-a-wares brought her to their village. She was well-treated and grew to like the ways of the Indians. She began to forget English.

95

Soon she could speak only the Indian language. She wore long wool Indian dresses. When she grew old enough, she married a Del-a-ware warrior. Finally, when the Del-a-wares camped near the Miamis, she learned to live with Miamis and finally married a Miami man when her first husband died.

All this time her family thought she was dead. When she was an old woman and the trader found her, she told him a little of her story. He wrote to her family back in Pennsylvania.

The letter reached her brother Joseph Slocum in 1837. Two of her brothers and a sister came to Indiana from Pennsylvania to see Francis.

They wanted her to go back with them to Pennsylvania, but she said she could not. She was all Indian now and wished to stay with her children on the Mis-sis-sin-e-wa. There she died in 1847. People visit her grave today near Peru.

And so, the Miamis watched the twentieth century come. The western part of the tribe lived in Oklahoma on the Qua-paw Reservation. There were other Indians there, Ott-a-was, Wy-an-dotts, Pe-o-ri-as. They had been neighbors in the Midwest, and now they were neighbors out west. The Miamis married with these other tribes and whites too. Soon there were very few full-blooded Miami Indians.

The Oklahoma Miamis farmed, growing grain. In 1940 the Oklahoma Miamis became a corporation. This meant they could make money as a group, pay taxes, and take care of their people just like a business.

In the 1950's this Miami corporation sued the U.S. government. The Miamis said the price they got for their Indian lands long ago in the treaty of St. Mary's was too low. The government agreed and gave the tribe over four million dollars. This seemed to be a fair price, finally, for the beautiful woodlands.

Francis Slocum was called the White Rose of the Miamis by pioneers when she was found living among the Indians.

The Miamis today who live in Oklahoma look like and are mostly farmers. Some have grown rich because zinc and lead, metals used by industry, were found on their lands.

In Indiana the story was a little different. On the last Indian reservation in the state, the Mis-sis-sin-e-wa, the Miamis could not get used to farming and didn't like it. Little by little they sold off their lands. Many were very poor.

When they went into the villages, everybody around them was white. Even in 1900 people were still looking down on the Miamis because they were different and also because the white people had always been afraid of Indians.

The Miamis felt the white people looked down on them. Some tried to forget they were Indians as fast as they could. Others were proud. Little by little, though, surrounded by white life, they forgot Miami language and customs. During that time they did seem to be a lost and forgotten people.

About 1910 Miamis in Indiana began to remember who they were. A new sense of pride began which continues even today. The great grandchildren of Miamis in Indiana are trying to get the government to name them as Miamis as it does the Oklahoma branch of the tribe.

There are Miami Indian offices in some towns now which take care of Indian affairs. How do people of Miami blood look to the future? With courage and pride in the past but hope for today and tomorrow.

So Little Turtle was right. He did believe that the Miamis could never be destroyed, that they would fall but rise from the earth they loved to bloom again, if they could learn to change. And if they kept their hearts right.

That is what they are doing today, a proud people learning to change and grow in a new age.

Gabriel Godfroy, a descendant of the chief, and George Durand Godfroy, near the turn of the century. (Used with permission of the Miami County Historical Society).

Miamis tried to become part of village life. Here they help celebrate an event in Peru in the early 1900's. Some wear western Indian head feathers, which were popular at the time. (Miami County Historical Society).

YOU AND YOUR FAMILY CAN LEARN ABOUT THE MIAMIS AND OTHER INDIANS BY VISITING INDIANA'S HISTORICAL MUSEUMS AND SITES

HISTORIC FORT WAYNE is a reconstructed fort and Indian encampment from 1816. It is located at 211 S. Barr in Ft. Wayne and is open from Mid-April to early November. At Historic Fort Wayne costumed settlers and Miami re-enacters show visitors how life was really lived in early Indiana.

Old Fort Wayne is operated by the Allen County-Fort Wayne Historical Society.

MORE INDIAN EXPERIENCES ...

The Miami County Historical Society in Peru has many artifacts (tools, letters, guns, and prehistoric Indian materials) of Miami Indians. In the picture (above right) a staff member works to help move to new quarters. A bust of Little Turtle is also shown.

The Tippecanoe County Historical Society is housed in the Moses Fowler House in Lafayette. Its Woodland Indian Gallery gives a glipmpse of the culture of this area from 10,000 B.C. to about 1838. The picture (above left) shows an interpreter explaining Mound Builders to school children.

Other Indian exhibits of many American tribes may be seen at the Museum of Indian Heritage, 6040 DeLong Road in Indianapolis.

The Indiana State Museum, The Children's Museum, Angel Mounds State Park, and the Indiana Experience at Union Station all have Indian materials for you to learn about and enjoy.

GLOSSARY OF
MIAMI INDIAN WORDS

A-MA-wi-a a-WA-ki	beehive
A-SON-da-ki Ca-IP-a-wa	Shining Morning Sun
A-PE-Kon-it	Jerusalem artichoke, the name of William Wells, a white boy who was captured by the Miamis and who later returned to the whites
a-KA-wi-ta	porcupine
a-LAN-ya	brave, young man
ci-ci-KWI-a	rattlesnake
Del-a-wares	Indians from the east who lived in Indiana at the time of this book
ka-SI-ta	ambush
ka-ka-TA ki-LANG-wi-a	butterfly
kwe-US-a	boy
KWANG-wa-SA	chipmunk
Ke-ki-ON-ga	Miami home village at Forty Wayne Indiana
ki-no-ZA-wia	panther
ko-KA	frog
kin-NIK-in-nick	aromatic herbs smoked by Indians
Ki-tchi-man-IT-o-wac	Great Serpent god
KICK-a-poo	an Indian tribe in eastern Indiana and Illinois

Le-ni-PIN-ja or Mi-ci-BI-si	Fire tiger spirit, supposed to dwell in rivers like the Mississinewa
Me-shi-kin-O-qua	The Little Turtle, great chief of the Miamis
min-dgi-pi	corn
MA-qua	bear
MOS-wa	deer
MAN-it-to (or Manitou or Mannito)	Indian spirit-god
Mis-sis-SIN-e-wa	River in central Indiana where Miamis lived
Mock-SIN-kic-kee	a lake in northern Indiana, Lake of Boulders
Nan-ah-BOOZ-hoo	Son of the West Wind in Indian myths
na-na-MAM-kic-kee	earthquake
NI-ka	friend
OK-sa	father
pas-QUAN-di-a	ball to play a game with
Pi-AN-ke-shaws	branch of Miami tribe living near Vincennes
Pot-a-WOT-a-mis	famous Indian tribe living in Indiana, Illinois and Michigan
SA-ki-a	crane bird
Shaw-NEES	A strong tribe of Indians living in Ohio and Indiana at the time of this book
tan-DAK-sa	bluejay
Tens-KWAT-a-wa	The Prophet, one of the Shawnee brothers who wanted Indians to drive out the whites in 1811
Te-CUM-seh	Brother of The Prophet, great leader of Indian peoples
Tip-pe-can-OE	River in northern Indiana, site of battle in 1811 between Indians and whites
WE-as	Branch of Miamis located on Wabash
We-mi-AM-iki	The Miamis, 'All beavers' or good folk
WI-nam-ac	an Indian leader, Potawatomi chief

THINGS TO SAY IN MIAMI INDIAN

'I'm climbing up'   'Ka-ka-ta WI-a-ni'
'I'm asleep'   'Na-pa-ni'
'I'm cooking'   'A-LI-mi TWA-ni'
'I'm eating'   'We-SI-ni i-an-ni'
'I see him'   'Na-wa-ka'
'I'm playing'   'PA-pi A-ni'
I'm cold'   'NIN-ji LAT-ci'

The Indiana Miami Council, active today as in the past, meets often to act on tribal matters.

The Hoosier Heritage Series focuses on events and people in Indiana History. Nancy Niblack Baxter teaches English at Cathedral School in Indianapolis.

ACKNOWLEDGEMENTS

I wish to thank the following people for their time and encouragement in this project:

Michael Hawfield, Director of the Allen County-Ft. Wayne Historical Society and Historic Ft. Wayne; Bill Wepler, Curator, Miami County Museum; Sheryl Hartman of Kekionga Indian Traditions; Amy Cox of the Indianapolis Public Schools; the staff of the Indiana Historical Bureau, particularly Dani Pfaff; Adeana Colvin of Garden City Elementary School; the staff of the Tippecanoe County Museum; and, finally, Lora Siders and her staff at the Miami Nation of Indians of Indiana in Peru.